LOWRIDER BLUES

LOWRIDER CLUBS

LOWRIDER BLUES
Cantando, Gritando y Llorando

A Compilation of Short Stories and Observations
from

My Inner Barrio
by

Marie Romero Cash

SANTA FE

*The 1964 Buick Electra on the cover belonged
to the author's father, Emilio R. Romero.*

Sunstone books may be purchased for educational, business, or sales
promotional use. For information please write:
Special Markets Department, Sunstone Press,
P.O. Box 2321, Santa Fe, New Mexico 87504-2321.

Book design ›Vicki Ahl
Body typeface ›Palatino
Printed on acid free paper

Library of Congress Cataloging-in-Publication Data

Cash, Marie Romero.
  Lowrider blues : cantando, gritando y llorando, a compilation of short stories and
observations from my inner barrio / by Marie Romero Cash.
     p. cm.
  ISBN 978-0-86534-704-5 (softcover : alk. paper)
  1. Hispanic Americans--Social life and customs--Fiction. 2. New Mexico--Fiction.
I. Title.
  PS3603.A8644L68 2009
  813'.6--dc22

                              2009009487

WWW.SUNSTONEPRESS.COM
SUNSTONE PRESS / POST OFFICE BOX 2321 / SANTA FE, NM 87504-2321 /USA
(505) 988-4418 / ORDERS ONLY (800) 243-5644 / FAX (505) 988-1025

Lowrider

A thousand pounds of shiny metal,
So smooth and sleek.
Moving along the boulevard, so low and slow.
Just fast enough to turn the wheels,
Barely crawling,
Barely rolling,
Taking it all in,
Warm hands fondle gleaming chrome.
So, is the lowrider the vehicle or the *vato* behind the wheel? Tatooed arms and body, folded bandana wrapped around long, sleek hair. Decorated hood, twirling hubcaps, gleaming bumpers wrapped around painted fenders.
Three *chicas locas* sit in the back seat. Ruby lips, jiggly bosoms. Everything moving up and down to the rhythm of oiled hydraulics.

Preface

Over the years I have discovered that almost every event in life contains a potential story. Not a day goes by that I don't see or hear something that sparks my interest, and I make a note of it. This is exactly how *Lowrider Blues* evolved, from observations I've been fortunate to witness. Some are poignant, some happy, some sad, and some so funny I couldn't believe my eyes. Observing life from the sidelines allowed me to notice sometimes insignificant details and subtle nuances. Sometimes I write about events that actually happened; or might have happened; or my perception of what I believe should have happened, so there is no sure way to tell if the story is real or imagined.

As I wrote these stories, I wanted to capture the essence of the people I grew up with: family, relatives, friends and acquaintances, and those strangers you meet on the street or the local hangouts. I have embellished facts and events by taking a small incident and gently feeding it to make it grow. There is a fine line between fact and fiction, and I have taken total advantage of it. Many times stories end as I would have imagined they would have ended, or should have ended, if they were indeed true.

I grew up in an era where Spanish was our language at home and English was our language at school. Consequently one overlapped the other and there was always a mix of Spanglish, if you will. I loved the way our language could be turned into combinations of words which could evoke laughter. (I've included a Glossary at the end of this book that the reader will find useful.) We all have watched "Valley Girls" from California and their enunciation of ordinary words. *Lowrider Blues* has its own Valley Girls, straight out of Northern New Mexico, but their tanned skin is natural and they have names like Myra and Esperanza, and they wear lots of makeup and like to crack their chewing gum as they discuss important events, such as nail polish and boyfriends.

I have gleaned a wealth of material from just looking around me—watching, observing. From these observations came the sounds and smells which ignited an interest in the final outcome. There have been times in my adult life where I was outraged at someone taking advantage of another person. Many of my stories are based on actual incidents which end with a proposed Karmic judgment of sorts: that the offender might not be punished here on earth, but they certainly will in the afterlife where they will meet up with the people they offended. With tongue in cheek, I rely on St. Peter at the Golden Gate to mete out the justice, as I know these culprits will have to face not only the Man Upstairs, but also those who have passed before them and know very well the dastardly deeds they performed here on earth.

My parents instilled in me a love of Santa Fe, our family and our culture. I hope I have been able to pay homage to that love they expressed so generously.

—Marie Romero Cash

LOWRIDER BLUES

1

Y ou know, it was before all the video stores came in. Even in *Peñasco*, where they opened one up right next to Ofelia's Restaurant. They even rented VCR machines to people who didn't own one or couldn't afford one.

My brother, Freddie, ran around with a bunch of lowrider *vatos*. Father Vincent told us we shouldn't equate these guys with gang members, because they just belong to local car clubs, not gangs. He said you shouldn't be calling them *Chollos*, either.

So Myra was curious why they all wore tattoos and walked like the old *pachuco* her Aunt Sally used to live with. He had tattoos all over, and he didn't look any different than these guys look now. And besides, Myra said, it was really freaky to be riding down the boulevard and have these guys surround you with their cars, pumping them up and down like they were having sex, and here you were in the middle.

—Oh, *greñuda*. Admit it. You just got the hots for that Nicolas. He drives that '78 Plymouth with all the chrome. And it's got that big old *Virgen de Guadalupe* painted on the hood, just like the tattoo on his back.

—No, but I think he's too cute, in a *macho* kind of way. His hair is so long and silky, and he likes for chicks to braid it all the way down his back.

—Yeah, but his eyebrows don't even stop in the middle, they just travel all the way across, like that Frida Kahlo chick.

—Oh, Mercy! You're just jealous of those eyelashes! Oh, man, he can flutter those at me anytime. And when he makes that little motion with his hand and his mouth says silent words, *call me*, I just want to melt.

—Sure, you and every chick from five miles around. Don't you know he's bad news? You remember how he treated Rosanna. Gets her all excited and pregnant and then she gives up her apartment and her job at the bank to go live in Vallecitos, up in the hills, where there's barely electricity, let alone gas. Freezing her ass off and shoveling snow all winter just so he can have a clean place to park his car. And so what does she get for all his kootchy koos and I love yous? A year later he takes up with another floozy, and moves her in upstairs while Rosanna and the baby still live downstairs; then she was shoveling snow for both their cars, what a stupid ass. So she finally leaves him, all heartbroken and everything, him standing there in his muscle shirt, showing his bulgy biceps, his arms around that skinny bitch, while Rosanna was putting her and the kid's stuff in that piece of shit station wagon he bought her from his settlement with the County.

—So Myra, don't go being stupid and thinking you can change this guy. I was watching Dr. Phil yesterday and he says these guys just don't change. He'll do to you what he did to Rosanna. There's always another one standing in line waiting to leave her butt print on his mattress. And besides, I saw that last one hanging on to Julio at the Allsup's, so she's already old news.

—Okay, little sister, I get the message. But that don't mean he ain't hot!

—So is salsa, *stupida*, but sometimes it will rip you a new one!

2

And did you hear what happened to Auntie Julia? She's in the poorhouse now, and, *pobrecita,* she doesn't even know who she is or how she got there.

I heard it from my cousin Joseph. I saw him at the Wal-Mart the other day and I couldn't find the candles and we were standing in the aisle talking and he told me the whole story. Well, you remember how Auntie was getting old and she had all these health problems, but none of them were very serious except maybe the diabetes, and they were always taking her to *La Clinica* to keep her blood sugar regulated. Anyway, everyone in the family had jobs either in Los Alamos or Santa Fe and nobody could stay home and take care of her, and her old man died last year, Uncle Fito, and so they kept getting these women to come and take care of her but then they wouldn't stay very long because they wanted to get paid thirty dollars an hour, like if they were nurses, or something, and they didn't know shit, so they'd leave and the family would be running back and forth trying to take care of her. Well, Auntie was an old sweetheart, no trouble at all, just a little on the feeble side. She had most of her marbles, but she was real forgetful, and every time I went to visit, she'd tell me to have some cake, and there never was any, so I'd just eat whatever I found in the fridge.

So then, her daughter Denise is almost ready to retire from her job at the school district and she figures if each one of the family will pay her thirty dollars a week, between that and her retirement check from the schools she can pay her bills and come to live with Auntie and take care of her.

So everything is going fine, a year or so passes, and you know that family, they visit whenever, and Auntie looks fine to them, she's clean and she's eating good and the house looks nice, so they figure

Denise is doing an okay job, and what the hell, for thirty dollars a week they don't have to keep making that hundred and sixty mile trip every few days. Besides the grandkids don't like to visit because Auntie doesn't have cable or a computer or anything and her house is real small and you can't flush the toilet paper down the toilet when you use it; you have to put it in the trash can next to the sink, and that's really gross, and they start to get on each other's nerves.

Well, Denise didn't have a boyfriend or anything ever since that *gargaho* she was married to for twenty five years ran off with the lady bus driver from the deaf school. So she always took Auntie on little trips to get away from the walls closing in on them. They even went to Las Vegas and stayed at the Hard Rock Hotel. Auntie Julia thought the lights were real pretty. And they would go to California and to Arizona once in a while, just for a few days and just to get away when it was snowing too much around here. The family thought that was real nice, especially since *they* never thought of taking her anywhere, especially after Uncle Fito died, he used to take her all over, to the store and to church and even to the little league games to watch the grandkids play.

Well somewhere during the last six months, Denise started being real secretive about money, saying everything was fine and she already balanced the checkbook and put it away and couldn't remember where right now but next time you come it will be right here I'm sure. And every time one of the kids called or came to visit there was nobody home, and the last time Joseph came he waited until nine o'clock when he heard Denise's car coming up the driveway. She was surprised to see him and he asked where they'd been, so late and everything, and she said they went shopping at Cottonwood Mall in Albuquerque and by the time they ate and everything, it was late. Well Joseph goes to hug Auntie goodnight and she smells like cigarette smoke and since none of them smoke, he asks Denise and she says they were sitting next to a bunch of smokers at Garduno's, and Joseph knows they don't let you smoke, especially in Albuquerque, where they have a law. On the way out he goes to grab his keys from the table and sees a little paper tag on her car keys, it's a valet parking thing from the casino down the road.

Well he doesn't say anything and goes home and tells his wife about it, and the next day Ruthie calls her other sister-in-law and she gets all riled up and decides to check the parking lot of the casino the next time they're not home. Sure enough she sees Denise's car and goes into the casino. She finds Auntie first, sitting in front of a Wheel of Fortune machine, a bucket of nickels in her hand, putting them in one by one, staring into the machine like she was freakin' hypnotized. Around the corner sits Denise, smoking a big old cigarette and putting silver dollars into a Triple Seven slot machine, talking to the old guy sitting next to her who's trying to borrow five dollars. Well, Pearl goes straight home and calls all the brothers and sisters and tells them the news, and a couple of them say so what, as long as Auntie's happy there's nothing wrong with them going to the casino, even if they go every day—the buffet is pretty good and besides it's cheaper than eating at home. But Pearl decides to carry it one step further. The next day she calls her friend Lucie who works at the bank and even though she's an officer and knows Pearl has no business looking at a bank account that she doesn't sign on, they've been friends ever since high school, so she makes a bunch of copies for her and asks if her brother Ivan is going out with anybody right now. Pearl goes home after stopping at the Taco Bell and while she's eating her Taco Supremes she starts to go through the bank statements one by one. So far so good. Groceries, bills, a few small cash withdrawals, probably for gas on one of their trips. But wait a minute, *dammit*, look at all of these withdrawals, and guess where from? You're right. The casino.

So it turns out that Denise was taking Auntie to the casino every day and spending all of Auntie's money, not that there was so much but it was all she had, and there was nothing left, not even enough to pay the light bill. And to top it off, Denise wasn't even sorry, she was all indignant like they didn't know what they were talking about, they're just jealous cause she's retired.

So the family has a meeting, without her, of course, and they decide to call the cops and make her pay up; but shit, she ain't got no money, except her retirement and that's only eight hundred bucks, and sure, if they got that every month, it would take five years to pay off what she gambled away, and then, get this, she said she was spending her own money and Auntie was the one doing all the gambling. And you know Auntie, she don't know a casino from a church. So finally, she got away with it because the police wouldn't do anything if Auntie didn't press charges since it was her money that went down the tubes. So she's *persona non grata* and nobody's talking to her, and Uncle Fito's probably rolling around in his grave. And do you know, that damned Denise still goes to the house to take Auntie to the casino? My treat, she says.

3

My cousin Gilbert served in the Vietnam War. But he don't like to talk about it, like it was some nightmare that he dreams over and over. He has these big dark circles under his eyes, and sometimes when he looks at you he's not even in the room. I never knew why he's on some kind of disability from the Government, but it don't look like nothing but his mind is in pain.

He was proud to be a Marine, his old beat up green U. S. Forest Service truck still has bumper stickers on it that say *Semper Fi* all these years later.

I don't think he really ever even came home. He's still over there in Nam, lying in a trench, soaked up to his ears in human mud.

4

Gina had her first lost weekend when she was fourteen. She got so rolled she didn't ever want to come down. And she didn't. Eventually she was freebasing up and down the entire West Coast and she didn't even know she had ever left Santa Fe. There's a lot she didn't know, like she was already four months pregnant from the Black dude she'd been with, cooking crack laced with baking soda. The kid turned out to be a present for her mother's forty second birthday.

5

My friend Alice hates getting old. Every birthday passes by and new wrinkles populate the fringes of her mind. She can't believe how old she's gotten, *why it was only yesterday* that she turned the head of every guy in the room, with her amethyst eyes and porcelain skin, and her eyebrows all perfectly arched. Now all the men, including her *gringo* husband, have gone off to younger pastures, hanging with women whose looks are but a passing thing and they too will watch from the sidelines as a younger chick infringes on their territory.

What is age, but a sliver in the log of time, Amiga? Consider the alternative: not all that sweet, either.

She tells me, don't worry, you'll be there too, and you'll know exactly how I feel, mark my words. It won't be long before you're counting all the wrinkles and pulling out gray hairs by the hundreds. I wave as I get on my bike and ride away, the orderly pushes her wheelchair back into the home, back into the loneliness of her years.

6

The long-legged chick with the turquoise eyes plucked his soul right out of his chest, sang a pretty song to it and then walked her six-inch heels all over his heart. And now he can't find his way home.

7

He cried out in agony, this brother of mine, when the liquor wrapped its arms around him, took him prisoner and wouldn't let him go.

His sorrow melted the air surrounding him, creating a wall of armor even Goliath couldn't penetrate.

And so we stood, out in front of the treatment center, debating whether to go in or not, me pushing, him pulling.

Maybe later, not now, I can't.

So we walked back down the crowded halls, where potential patients stood wishing they too could walk away; away from the promised relief into its certain agony.

He looked at me with his soulful eyes, as though waiting for me to knock some sense into him. But I knew I could never play the role of some high-handed judge, and I swallowed two more Valiums, just enough to make it home.

8

I've noticed lately that a lot of people I know don't go to church anymore. So what's this stuff the *DaVinci Code* talks about, that Jesus was married to Mary Magdalene and that she was pregnant at the Crucifixion, and that they had a daughter named Sarah?

Who thinks up this stuff? Why can't we just believe that God happened and all is good. No reason to put another spin on the story.

So why don't you go to church? Because you have your God within you and you don't need a church to worship in? *Because everybody there is a hypocrite, worshiping on Sunday and screwing everybody over on Monday?* Or is it because what did God ever do for me? And maybe you think there's a universal church where everything you do is judged from within. There's more excuses, I know, but I can't remember them right now.

I stopped going because of guilt. Guilt that every little thing I did wrong was being wracked up on a big scoreboard. Guilt that thinking about things was of itself a sin, and I couldn't figure that out because you were guilty before you committed the act—and that was too hard to fathom. If you thought about sex, you were guilty of sex, especially without marriage. Well guess what, it doesn't look like marriage is an option right now, and besides, who made that stupid rule—think it and you've done it?

I stopped going because priests we respected were doing things to make us lose respect. Because priests are supposed to be holier than us. I quit going because I got tired of going, and did I notice anything different? You're damned right I did. My life started crumbling at the edges, my finances went to hell, and the family dramas became larger than life, pulling me in all directions. And confession seemed farther away than ever—but why was it necessary anyway, having thought of going, shouldn't that have been enough?

9

The *vato* tells the story about how bad off he was, into the booze and crystal meth and women, and the horror of it all. And how everything got all screwed up and he didn't know if he was coming or going. And he's told the story so many times, and now that's all he is, is the story. He plays the part and talks the talk, pushing rehab to all the *vatos* who fall by the wayside; and how his blessed mother, God rest her soul, knelt down in front of her little home altar with all the candles lit and the fresh lilacs in the Mason jar, and prayed to St. Anthony to save her son. And that now he's better, he's learned the lesson, walked the walk, and everyone pats him on the shoulder and wishes they could be like him. But in the deepness of the dark, the nightmares keep him cornered, screaming to wake up in the comfort of his mother's arms again.

10

My Momma was married to an Indian. I don't believe my father ever loved Momma, at least not like what we saw on television. He shied away from crowds and family gatherings, and in a crowd of Indians, he pretended not to be with us, but mostly not with her. She was what they now call "Hispanic," but was whiter than most. At least with us he could pass us off as relatives rather than family, but she didn't look like anybody who lived out there in the sun. I noticed he never held her hand or was affectionate in any way, especially when other people were around. He would shrug away whenever she patted him affectionately, or reached up to gently brush something from his face, or asked if he needed anything.

There were lots of times he didn't come right home after work. Momma would assure us he was working late, but I wasn't stupid. Nobody worked eighteen hours at a stretch, at least not in our neighborhood. I watched one night as she paced the floor, wiping the kitchen counter for the hundredth time, scraping the now dry dinner into a plastic container. She came into the living room and said, with forced enthusiasm, *let's go get some ice cream, guys!* And we all piled into the truck. Before we got there, though, she said she wanted to stop somewhere for a minute. We went a little ways up the highway and turned into a parking lot full of cars and trucks, but mostly trucks. There were lots of people milling around, talking and drinking beer. Loud country music blared through the open doors of the building. Billows of smoke wove their way from the top of the crowd out into the night air. Two men and a woman were laughing and giggling in the next car, playfully fighting over a bottle of whiskey. I noticed they were Indians. In fact, most everybody around looked mostly Indian. They were off the rez—drinking and dancing in the middle of suburbia.

Mom rolled the windows up almost to the top and said, *Stay here, don't move, I'll be right back.* The usual admonition reserved for all parking lots and malls came next. *Don't open the doors, don't talk to anyone,* and *don't follow me. I'll be right back.* I watched as she walked the short distance to the entrance, ignoring the whoops and catcalls from the guys standing near the door. *Hey baby, slow down...talk to me...what's your name...wanna dance?* She sidestepped them and then was lost in the smoky crowd.

After what seemed like an awfully long time, I started to get scared. I wasn't too sure what we were doing there, and the music was getting louder and louder. *Way more than listening to KBUZZ on the radio.* I kept looking straight at the door hoping she would magically appear, but she wasn't coming out, and the crowd kept getting bigger as more cars filed into the already burgeoning parking lot. My attention was riveted on the door, but it was diverted when I heard a loud crash right in front of my eyes. A big Indian driving a beat-up Ford pickup rammed the back end of an old Buick waiting for a parking space. Both drivers jumped out and began yelling blame. It looked to me like they were going to throw blows right there. The big Indian with the long black braid looked up at me and then came to the window and motioned for me to roll it down. Scared shitless, I cracked the window open only about an inch, making sure his big hand couldn't fit through that small space. He put his face right up to the window and said, *Hey Kid. What did you see? He hit me, right? He bashed right into my truck?*

Gee, I don't know, mister. I was asleep, I lied.

Shit, he muttered, and walked back. By this time the other driver had hauled ass. I saw him jump into his truck and head out in the same direction.

Meanwhile, it seemed as though my mother was taking way too long to do whatever she didn't tell me she was doing. I told my little sister to sit on the floor and not do anything and I would be right back with some candy. She looked at me with her big soulful eyes, and I handed her some gum I picked up at State Farm when we went to pay the insurance. I rattled the little box with their insignia, so she could see there was stuff inside. Assured I had her attention on these goodies, I patted her head and told her I'd be right back, and quietly closed the truck door behind me, making sure to push down the lock. I knew I would have hell to pay if my mother came back before I found her. I didn't want anyone to see me, so I stayed close to the other vehicles, working my way toward the entrance. A pack of dogs in a red pickup scared the hell out of me as I crept past them. I spun around so fast I lost my balance and almost fell over.

I reached the open doors of the building, overcome for a moment with the smell of smoke and alcohol and the heat generated by so many people. As I stood in a crowded corner, something caught my attention...a tall beauty of a young woman with deep indigo black hair. Her straight white teeth sparkled as she smiled up at *who*, my father, who looked down at her with the smile of someone eyeballing the dessert cart at Denny's Restaurant. Her purple velvet top became one with his pinstriped western shirt as their silver belt buckles clanked against each other. So I'm standing there watching my father slow dancing to the music, with someone I've never seen before. Can't even say it was a relative. She was looking at him all dreamy eyed, like he was a slice of chocolate cake. For a minute there, everything was moving slow and easy. The end of the music snapped me back to the task at hand, which was finding Momma and getting her back to the parking lot. I sure didn't want her to see this. I kept looking around but couldn't spot that shock of red hair of hers. Dad was taking a good swig of beer, sitting at a table with this woman and another couple when the music started up again. *Achy Breaky Heart*, I think it was. They played this song at all the rodeos we went to. Dad was up again, with the rest of the table, forming a dance line. In about a split second, I saw my mother get in the line right behind them, keeping right up with the tempo of the music. Everybody coupled up to sashay out to the middle of the floor, she stepped between my dad and this woman, grabbed his hands as if to dance with him, and said sarcastically, *Oh, excuse me! I mistook you for my husband! You look so much like him. But you couldn't be, he's at work.* As she spun around to walk away, she almost knocked me over. I grabbed her hand and we headed for the door. I could hear the guitars twanging out another she done me wrong song into the night air. In that instance

I also heard the sound of her heart breaking, shattering like an Acoma pot tumbling from a shelf and falling to the ground. I listened in silence as each tiny fragment found its way to the floor, immediately crushed to powder by the dancers whose shuffling cowboy boots mashed them into the sawdust.

As I glanced back, he didn't bother to follow us into the parking lot but decided instead to return to the revelry of his table, where he presided as chief. We reached the truck and got in, and she started to chew on my ass for having left BeeBee alone, who was fast asleep, her thumb fixed securely into her chubby lips, wrapped in a blanket of comfort known only to four-year olds. The words drifted off into the night air, as the engine ignited with a loud hum, and we pulled out of the parking lot into the star studded darkness.

I was no comfort to this mother of mine, who stared down the highway as though she was in a foreign land. As we neared the ice-cream store, I feigned a stomach ache and asked if maybe we could just go home, hoping that this small contribution might help ease her pain. I felt my youngness at that moment and wished I could magically become older and wiser. The small talk I made on the way home garnered no response, so we traveled the last miles home in empty silence.

11

I counted them up a while back—all the guys I'd ever dated. It surprised me that the number was so high. I always thought I was a wallflower. As I made a quick review, it dawned on me that none of them were real. Each time I had only imagined they were the one, the true love, the white knight, the elusive love I had looked for in all the wrong places.

And why was it necessary to fantasize, he asked, with his PhD in hand. *I don't see the reason for the need to make them something they weren't.* My response was simple, neither did I. I was marinated in the pleasure of being someone I was not. Oh, don't get me wrong, there was no raving beauty here, no long-legged vixen, but enough of *something* to attract these erstwhile men. I don't know. They were mostly a mix of musky aftershaves, clean cut and gentle-manly. I was well versed in the fantasy of them enjoying my company, and I theirs.

Ah, euphoria. Those first kisses were very special indeed. What if I never experience that feeling again?

12

The foundation crumbled many times, dropping her defenses to the ground, forcing her to wallow in guilt and misery, bathing her in two cups of sorrow mixed with one cup of fear. She returned many times wanting, hoping, wishing to conquer, determined to win, to cut her losses. Over and over she gathered her pennies, her quarters, her dollars, and took it all down the highway, to the place of magic lights and spinning reels, ready to beat the odds, to bring it all home. And the magic hole dug itself deeper as the plastic card with the secret password repeatedly spit out paper dollars, swelling the debt to fearful heights. Each day she swore to never return but the magic tentacles searched her out and wrapped themselves around her and dragged her there again and again with promises of redemption, everybody's a winner! *This time. Next time. Once again. Come on. You can do it.* And the downhill ride continued until the final wake-up call—the morning of the funeral, where one by one bewildered friends stood up and spoke of her kindness, her generosity, her thoughtfulness. But nobody spoke of her secret life amidst the flashing lights inside the casino walls.

13

My mother used to call them *Las Ricas*. Anglo women who had so much money they did nothing but shop for new clothes and volunteer at the museums. Their hands didn't show the wear and tear of women who worked every day and raised seven children too. Their slim bodies with not an ounce of fat were covered with designer labels decorated with layers of turquoise and silver necklaces, belts and bracelets, while we sucked our stomachs in so they wouldn't hang over too-tight jeans bought on sale at Wal-Mart.

Kissing the air near their cheeks as they greeted each other, they sat and talked about their travels to distant places, as fingers laden with gold and gems caught the light from the window nearby as they gestured grandly. And they talked above one another, anxious to hear their own voice tell of faraway New Delhi, Kurastan, Kashmir and Pakistan, and the fabulous hotels where they'd all stayed.

Botoxed foreheads with nary a crease, blonde hair with nary a wisp of gray, and plastic smiles from collagen-stuffed lips. I watched as each ate a few spoonsful, a bite of this, a bite of that, barely enough to sustain a small bird, and they were full, the wine having filled all the spaces in between. They continued to talk, of orchids, of wisteria, and then their heads bent forward in unison. Who was it they were discussing, in whispered tones? *Perhaps some indiscretion of a husband or a lover, whose name surely I would not have known.*

14

You turned your back and walked away, as my heart stopped beating.

And there have been no other footsteps to trample on the grave you left.

The morning star has lost its brilliance. The flowers have lost their haunting scent.

The rain feels cold and harsh. It blends with salty tears as they fall together from eyes which have almost stopped seeing.

My phone gathers cobwebs, as it sits in silence.

I wondered why I gave you my soul, handing it to you like some dime-store trinket.

I awoke to the rumble of the thunder, my stomach growled in unison.

How long had it taken to again be hungry for life?

15

I gotta tell you about my cousin Wilma, who after all those years decided to throw her brother off the family land in Chupadero; land she hadn't set foot on for twenty years, even while her father grew old and decrepit and eventually withered away. But oh, don't worry, he wasn't alone. My cousin Billy took care of him to his dying day, changing his clothes every time he made a mess, and feeding him *atole* with a stainless steel baby spoon he found at the flea market. And *hell no*, it wasn't easy, because Uncle Juan was an independent old cuss; he didn't want anybody to help him, so he fought all the way. One time we found him sitting in his car in front of the Seven-Eleven on the highway. No telling how he got there, since he stopped driving ten years back when he ran over that old lady in front of the church. *Gracias a Dios*, he only suffered a broken arm. And without his glasses, he couldn't see for two feet in front of him. But there he was, dressed in his Sunday best, brown suit and white shirt with an equally old pinstriped tie, staring out into who knows where, waiting for who knows what. I called my cousin to come and get him, but he had just finished a joint and couldn't find his car. And you couldn't call his sister, Wilma, because she lived on the other side of the valley and ever since she had married that old fart Alejandro, who everybody said was older than Methuselah, she stuck to him like glue, just in case he might decide to leave her and take all his money with him.

As if the seven kids from Alejandro's previous marriage weren't enough to repopulate the valley, together they had a kid named Norbert, who was all grown up now. Funny thing, she already had two other kids when she met him, but her *Abuelita* had raised them and she never had to lift a finger. What was she going to do with this one? She didn't know shit about raising kids, and Alejandro wasn't going to stand for her shipping his kid off for someone else to raise. So I don't know how she made it through all those years, but she drank a lot of vodka and that must have helped. By now Norbert is about forty, and the apron strings around his ass are probably causing a rash, but he's a money hungry kind of person, having lost all his retirement shooting craps at the casino down the way and looking for a Plan B to secure his future, especially now that Alejandro had cut him off. Nothing like having to cry crocodile tears on your mother's shoulder to get a few bucks. *Pobrecito, mi hito*, she would say as she handed him a check. *Pobrecito my ass*, Alejandro would say under his breath, his lips so tight you could barely see the line. *Go out and work for a living like the rest of the world. I tell you, Wilma, you've got him so spoiled he's not ever going to leave home!*

And one day Alejandro didn't get up to feed the horses or even to use the bathroom, and Wilma didn't notice, because she was busy writing child support checks for Norbert's two ex-wives. It wasn't until the next day she realized she hadn't seen her *viejo* since the day before, and when she went to his room, the stench of death had already filled it. To make matters worse, the county coroner came and wouldn't let them move the body until he figured out how Alejandro had died, suspecting maybe one of them was getting tired of waiting for the golden goose to fall into the pond and drown. Finally the priest came to give the blessings, and they took the body to the mortuary. The whole town buzzed with rumors, but the medical examiner finally decided Alejandro had died in his sleep from a stroke caused by all the steaks and eggs he had eaten throughout his life, not to mention the freshly churned butter and cheese.

By the time the body was six feet under and the ground barely settled, Norbert went over to the Courthouse to get himself appointed executor of the will since his mother, *pobrecita mi mama*, was too distraught to handle it. Well it was here at the courthouse that Norbert discovered how much money the old man really had. *A la machina!* He whispered under his breath. Of course, it was all going to his sweet little *madrecita*, the most precious person in his life! No matter, he was the only true heir to these newly found riches, since his half-sisters had a different father, even though Alejandro had always treated them like his own. Somewhere in the mix, when the paperwork was all done and the money was safely in his mother's checking account at the bank in Taos, Norbert started asking questions about his *Abuelo's* house and figured his mother was entitled to get a share of that, too, so he'd better check into it.

Oh, no, mijo, she protested. *Billy took care of your Abuelo for the last twenty years, I couldn't do that. I have enough here to keep me comfortable. I don't need any more.* But it took only three weeks for Norbert to convince her that she had to do something now, before she got too old, after all she was already in her seventies and *Abuelo* had been dead for over five years now. So Norbert once again made his way to the county courthouse and got himself appointed to oversee *Abuelo's* estate. For sure there was no will to be found, but in this state the law was that when someone died without a will, everything they owned would be shared equally between the survivors, in this case his mother and Billy; and the probate judge, who was also the town plumber, didn't even ask what Norbert's interest was. He just had the clerk stamp his signature on everything Norbert presented and the wheels rolled into motion.

Billy was surprised to see Norbert at the front door one day that summer, since he hadn't even attended *Abuelo's* funeral because he couldn't get off work that day, holding a bunch of papers in his hand, which he started explaining without bothering to say hello first. *What the hell you mean,* Billy said, *you're in charge of what? He was my father, not yours, so take your papers and shove them up your skinny ass and get the hell off this property!* Billy was pretty pissed, and history reflected he could get violent without much provocation, so Norbert just threw the papers on the floor and took off with his *cojones* shaking. The next day the cleaning lady picked all the papers off the porch and placed them neatly on the kitchen table. At lunchtime, Billy was sitting there doing the crossword puzzle in the *Rio Arriba Times* when he glanced over and saw the word *Order* on the top page of the stack of papers. *Order, shit,* he said to himself and started reading. The judge had ordered that Billy allow that little bastard to inspect the premises and take an inventory. *Inventory's ass,* he said out loud. *What the hell was there to inventory? Ten years' worth of doctor bills, a hundred empty prescription bottles, and four* boxes of unused diapers? *Who the hell was Norbert trying to impress?* And to top it the hell off, Billy was ordered to pay a whole chunk of money if he wanted to keep driving *Abuelo's* old pickup truck, since Norbert had gone on the internet and figured it was worth over three thousand dollars. *Three thousand, my ass! Maybe if the damn thing had an engine that was worth a shit!*

Early the next morning, Billy went to see Ezekiel Rodriguez, the attorney at Valley Legal Aid, who told him he was sorry but the law said anyone could be appointed administrator of an estate, and since nobody else had taken the time to do so, the grandson had every right, since he was looking after his mother Wilma's interests. *What interests,* Billy shouted. *The only time she ever came over the whole ten years Dad was sick and senile, was on his birthday, and then she would only stay long enough to give him another flannel shirt and a pair of socks to add to the other twenty in the closet. I kept the place up. I added rooms to the house so we could have a little rent money; I took care of everything, and when he couldn't walk anymore, I carried him back and forth to the doctors. She never did shit for him and now she wants half? Bullshit! I'll burn the place down before I'll let that happen!*

Calma te! the attorney said. *Calm down! It's the law. Your father didn't leave a will. She gets half. You get half. End of story. You should have gotten your old man to give you a deed. That would have settled it!*

Billy explained, *he was going to but then we decided to wait, because my ex-wife was a bitch who would try to take it all away from me. We never expected him to die, and since I had added so much around the original house, including the barn and the corrals, I always figured it would be mine.*

But you have no proof of anything, the attorney retorted. *No judge in his right mind is going to rule in your favor without receipts, without proof.*

Well, dammit, she knows it, isn't that enough?

No, my son, it isn't. Call me in a couple of weeks. I'll get in touch with their attorney and see where it goes.

A few weeks later, Billy got a call from Ezekiel who said he had some good news and some bad news. The bad news was that his sister and Norbert wanted the property sold and split in half, or it could be appraised and Billy could pay Wilma her half in cash. The good news was that if the property was sold, his share would be over a hundred thousand dollars, and he could buy himself a little piece of land and a house somewhere in the valley.

Billy didn't even hang up the phone. He just fell to his knees and cried, not in thanksgiving, but in sorrow. Across town, Norbert convinced his mother they should transfer her share to a joint account, just in case.

And what happened to Billy, you ask? Well, the last time I saw him he was sitting in his truck in front of the courthouse, staring out into who knows where, and thinking who knows what, a check from the title company clutched in his hands, his share from the sale of the house he had lived in all his life, his truck loaded with miscellaneous stuff he gathered, including some old photos of his parents, and the walking stick he carved from a cottonwood branch when his father was starting to get a little wobbly on the feet. And as for Norbert, the last time I saw him, he was taking the shuttle to catch a Southwest Airlines flight to Las Vegas, having just recently buried his mother, *Pobrecita, God rest her soul*. And as I drank my morning coffee a day or two later, the headlines of the paper in front of me told of a jet airplane that had crashed in the mountains of Northern New Mexico, shortly after departing Albuquerque on its way to Las Vegas, the lone fatality having been a man in his forties from a small village north of Santa Fe whose identity was being withheld until the family could be notified.

16

The eight-o'clock service on Sunday at St. Francis Cathedral is a Spanish mass. All the old folks and the regulars sit in one of the two chapels, and the visiting tourists and young families sit in the main part of the church. I myself sit in the La Conquistadora Chapel, but I'm not sure whether I'm considered a regular or one of the old folks. Sometimes there's a Mariachi mass, with lively guitar music that makes you want to dance right there in your pew; but most of the time there's a choir, led by a young woman whose voice reaches heights most singers only aspire to.

Most times I sit behind couples. Very rarely are there men alone, but always women alone, and always couples. Sometimes I sit behind or next to a tall man with ruddy skin and gentle eyes. His silver gray hair is streaked with threads of white. He bends over gently to smooth a flyaway hair on his wife's face, and her eyes light up in momentary recognition and she smiles up at him. She's a petite woman, with olive skin and dark unruly hair. An unlikely couple by today's standards, most might say, but probably childhood sweethearts. They're old school, hard core Catholics, Spanish to their roots, and as the choir sings and the prayers are recited, their voices are united. Spanish words and syllables pronounced with certainty, as I struggle to read the prayers from the book, stumbling with each barely familiar word.

She kneels, almost tipping the pew in front of her as he quickly reaches for her. And when she tries to stand on disobedient legs, he gently helps her up. Sometimes she dozes off during the sermon and her head inclines towards his ready shoulder. Gently, ever patient, he shakes her awake; reminding her they're still in church. She remembers the ritual; she remembers the prayers, the songs of Glory to God. But what her tortured mind does not remember are him, her, and why.

17

The whistling wind ripped through the stillness. The chimes hanging in the porch furiously clanked their metallic edges. Window panes opened and shut to the rhythm, and curtains flailed wildly, their shadows flickering on dimly illuminated walls. The waxy scented candles had long spent their last glow as I sat in the darkness, clutching the tattered rabbit Auntie Mela had sent oh so many years ago, fifty to be exact. I could feel my heart racing, my stomach churning, but yet I didn't want to move. Not all the sounds in the room were from the wind, which continued to whirl through even the cracks in the door. My thoughts were pushing noisily against the inside of my head. How I hated winter. And even more than that, I hated being sick.

The power had gone out yesterday. Inches of snow blanketed the ground. I watched as my chest rhythmically moved up and down with each breath. I still had the pounding headache I went to bed with. I glanced out the window again, wishing some miraculous event would take this all away, and prayed fervently to the little statue next to my bed. The headaches had returned about the time I began to see a therapist regularly, where I began to slowly untangle the threads of my life. I rummaged through the night stand, looking for the extra bottle of Tylenol. The clock noisily ticked the minutes away: two, three, four o'clock. No sunrise yet. Outside, the snow covered car in the driveway blended into the all-white background. I took a sip of the hours old tea and dropped my head back against the pillows. For an instant I was back home, with Mother sitting on the edge of the bed rubbing Mentholatum on my chest, until the pungent waxiness soaked into my skin. Even then I noticed the subtle creases which had begun to creep into her face. Gray wisps of once-black hair hung loosely from her brow. How had this tiny woman raised seven children and still maintained her sanity. *Or had she?*

It had been a while since I'd traveled the seventy miles to the home where Mother had resided for months over three years—a cheerfully sunny place with cheerfully sunny nurse's aides and cheerfully sunny rooms. There Mother sat in the middle of the parlor, oblivious to her surroundings and temporarily enchanted by a loose white thread clinging to her crisp denim pants. She watched as her long wiry fingers patiently stroked her pant leg until the thread finally surrendered. Seconds later she was slumped over, adjusting the Velcro on her white leather Reeboks. This too, she approached with endless patience, pulling the strap, then aligning it, then pulling it again. An aide touched her arm and asked if she was thirsty, holding a half-filled glass of orange liquid in her hand. She looked up, wide-eyed, smiled, and then returned to the business of Velcro. The aide gently pulled her up from a scrunched position and straightened her back. The cold liquid was tart, but she drank it anyway. What was that familiar taste? Where did it come from? A fleeting moment of recognition, *good juice*, she whispered as her gaze shifted to the television set sitting in silence in the middle of the room, black and white figures locked in endless motion. She watched the other inmates of this prison and found it odd that everyone was in a wheelchair or a walker. Next to her the tall lady slept, folded forward like a pretzel, oblivious as the aide dutifully mopped the floor around them.

Where are my things? she thought, looking at her empty hands. Meticulously applied nail polish streaked the tips of her fingers, stark crimson against the whitish skin which rarely saw the sun. The day moved slowly forward. Somewhere down the hallway someone talked about the redemption of the Lord, *it must be Sunday.* A captive audience listened as the large bespectacled man read from a red leather-covered book. Did he really believe *these* souls needed saving? She looked up as a smiling figure walked toward her. She smiled too, as her eyes took on a familiar sparkle. *I know this person,* she thought, *but who is it? Oh look, a butterfly. Maybe I can touch it.* The now stranger hugs her bony arms and asks her how she feels. *Does she feel? Does she think? Can she think? Why can't she think? Why am I here? Where's my husband? Where's my family?*

Where's my house? Ah, there's that thread again, and she bends over in her chair to once again resume the battle.

The dinner tables are set with dark green table cloths and matching napkins. The aroma of freshly cooked food fills the room. The lady next to her reaches across the table, grabs her glass and drinks from it. The aide gently takes it and returns it. The brown haired woman reminisces of evenings in New York and the Bolshoi Ballet she attended oh so many years before, and of Tiffany's where her husband bought her the most beautiful ring. The tall lady is awake now, but her medicine has worn off, just about the time the blonde nurse comes in with small white cups of relief mixed with chocolate pudding. Each mouth gets a loving spoonful and moments later things are calm again.

Her fork wanders through orange, white and brown mounds of food, blended into a tasteless mush. For a moment she recalls the taste of pinto beans and green chili, scooped up by warm flour tortillas fresh off the grill, but that memory quickly disappears. As night falls the aides prepare them all for bed, and the slumber of the innocents. The aide pulls the tightly knit orange comforter over her chest and strokes her forehead, telling her to sleep tight and don't let the bedbugs bite. As she closes her eyes, she feels a strange pressure in her chest, and falls asleep adjusting her pillow as the aide quietly leaves the room.

Outside my window, the wind continues to push unyielding branches against the plastered adobe walls of my modest home. It is finally daybreak. I get up slowly, moving my head to see if by some miracle my headache has subsided. It has. I glance toward the window. The wind has stilled. A blanket of snow rests gently on the ground, as the sun peeks out from behind gray clouds. A small bird jumps from branch to branch of the leafless apricot tree next to the bedroom wall, pecking rhythmically at the window as if tapping out a Morse-code message. I listen intently as it continues the tap-tap-tapping, surprised it does not move as I come closer. I am startled by the shrill ring of the phone.

Yes, hello, I say. *It is the home,* the voice on the other end says *your mother passed on peacefully during the night, just a couple of hours ago.* As I glance toward the window, I see the messenger has flown away.

18

Whisperings

The wind travels fast in the middle of the desert. Fast like
    lightning.
Lifting boy child like a feather.
Inside the whirlwind he spun.
Spinning. Spinning. Spinning.
Out of control. Like an old rag doll.
Wringing out his soul.
And then it stopped.
And dropped him to the ground.
With malice. Harshly.
He ran all the way home.
Faster. Faster. Faster.
Never stopping even to breathe.
And none of us ever understood why
He never came out of his mind.

19

*N*ow *don't you go buying your dad any booze*, she said, clinging to a moist handkerchief, well, paper towel, in her right hand. *You know he's been drinking way too long this time and he needs to stop, and I can't take it any more. This man is going to drive me crazy.*

I was just a kid, torn between two adults. A father who fought a battle every day with alcohol; and a mother who was never able to walk away from him. So what was I supposed to do? My dad was this big *vato* with tattoos all over his back and chest and he could kick your ass just by saying he would. He had this one eye that followed you around the room even when he wasn't looking at you. My mom was this tiny little *Gringa* person who met him at a Harley-Davidson rally in Las Vegas about fifteen years ago, and in her mind she left him every year about this time. Sometimes when I came home from school she would be unpacking her suitcase, even though she'd never even gone out the door. What I never knew was if she was going to leave me behind.

Uncle Lupe was my dad's older brother, and he ran a little liquor store in the Seven-Eleven across town. I could walk in there anytime and tell him my dad wanted a bottle of tequila and he never questioned me about it. He told me I had to be real discreet because he could lose his license selling to a minor, so I would get some bread and potato chips and put them in a big bag and he would slip the bottle into it when nobody was looking. A lot of times I would go there for a few days in a row and he would say, *que va, your old man's really tying one on this time,* and I would just nod my head in mutual agreement and then go down a few blocks into the park downtown and sell the half-pints to some of the winos. This way I always had money in my pocket, especially if my mom decided to leave me behind on one of her imaginary trips I could at least go to McDonald's and eat, 'cause my dad wasn't going to get up and fix us something to eat, ever.

I didn't know how to answer her. I didn't want to be disrespectful. I know he never asked *her* to go get his liquor, and he was smart enough not to drive in that condition after paying an attorney mega bucks a couple of times to get him off the DWI charges on the tickets he got. But shit, what was I supposed to do. Let him sit in that raggedy-ass chair for the rest of the day, pissing and moaning about how miserable his life had been, begging like a little kid for someone to *please, please* help him? And he didn't mean *help* him as in stopping drinking, he meant help him as in go get me a bottle and then I'll start cutting down. And besides, if I said no I knew it was going to make him mad enough to either throw something at me or chase me around the block, like he did that time when I was extra-cocky and told him to kiss my ass 'cause I wasn't going to ever buy him another bottle. He got up from that damned chair, wobbled for a second and then grabbed the baseball bat and started chasing me around the room. I thought he was just kidding until I saw that crazed look in his eyes, so I took off running out the door and down the street, and believe it or not, he was right behind me, running barefoot in a foot of snow, hollering at me to stop or I was going to be sorry. I was scared shitless, so I kept running and got far enough ahead to look back and see him stop and bend forward to catch his breath. Well in a few minutes I heard the sirens coming down our street and figured one of the neighbors had called the cops. I just told myself the hell with it and kept on running until I got to my friend Albert's house and he was real sympathetic because his dad was pretty much the same way, so we went into his garage and sat on the two old couches, listened to some rock music and lit up a couple of joints. Before long we were rolling on the floor laughing about the way my old man must have looked running down the street, freezing his feet off, with no shirt on and his unbuckled belt flying in the wind. Serves him right, getting his ass hauled off to jail. Of course they couldn't file any charges because I wasn't about to tell them it was me he was chasing, so they just kept him a couple of hours, let him sober up, and then drove him home. I waited until I knew he was asleep before I snuck in the house through the window of my room.

So now my mom is standing in front of me with her arms crossed and tapping her foot repeating that I'd better not go get him a bottle, and I'm nodding my head back and forth trying to figure out what to do. I know that if I do, she will never trust me again, and if I don't, he will make my life more miserable than it already is. I just wished everything could be normal. So I just went back to my room, packed up my mind and left, my mother crying and asking me what I was doing, and my dad hollering for me to get over here, and I just walked out of my life and never went back.

20

I saw you, after all these years
And I wanted to stop time
To step back into the path we had taken
Before you took the right fork and I took the left
Before you stopped loving me
Before you stopped trying
Before I stopped crying.

21

Who were all those old people?
With graying hair and wrinkled skin
Who struggled with every step as if in great pain
When did they become so old and frail
Just yesterday they were young and virile
Who is that person who stares back in the mirror
With trails of lines on skin that sags
With faded eyes that squint in the sunlight
Bones that creak with every step
The person inside them is still young
Who yearns to run and jump and play
To scream with joy over sweet candy and butterflies
Who are all those old people?
Could one of them be me?

22

"**Y**ou ain't no raving beauty, Estrella. So you need to rely on your brains. No man's going to want you, so you *gotta* get a good job and take care of your own self."

"That's really cruel, *Viejo*. You shouldn't say stuff like that to her."

"Well, look at her. She don't look like no Elizabeth Taylor to me. She looks like your Mother's side of the family, *Vieja*. Her teeth are crooked, she's fat, and her skin feels like sandpaper. No man's going to want her hanging around. *No*, she's better off finishing school and getting a job with the State. That way we don't have to worry about her. But *Gloria's* another story, *Vieja*. She looks more like you. All them guys chasing her around, she'll be married in no time!"

"She's only sixteen, *Hombre*! Don't go marrying her off. Besides, good looks don't mean nothing! Under all that makeup she's just another plain Jane. Estrella just doesn't like to put all that greasy stuff on her face. She says it makes her look unnatural. And she'd rather study than go out *crusing* with Gloria and her friends."

"Well, she'd *better* put something on her face or we're going to have her living with us until she's fifty."

"*Aieee!* You people act like I'm not even in the room. You just wait and see, Papa. I'm going to show all of you."

And so she did. Estrella eventually graduated from the university with a degree in marketing and married a fellow she met while studying for her master's degree at UCLA in California. And years later when she came home with her husband and teen-aged children for a short visit, there was Gloria, all fat and puffy, eating Doritos from the bag, her fourth husband sitting on the couch next to her, drinking the last few cans from the case of Budweiser he started that morning before the Dallas Cowboys game.

Her father stood next to the kitchen table, mixing up a batch of commodity eggs with powdered milk and making toast with welfare butter, trying hard to impress Estrella and her family.

23

*Q*ue Paso con todos los abogados? What happened to all those young attorneys? Where did they go, those erstwhile men, who pored through eight years of books to earn that coveted degree; who opened offices with equally jaded friends hoping to become the Perry Masons of their decade? Where did all those pretty secretaries come from, and the not so pretty one who did all the work, watching with shaded eyes as she saw their wives approach, knowing well the *do not disturb* sign meant just that. And he stood up quickly as his wife walked in, the pretty secretary holding the shorthand tablet over her chest, just high enough to cover the unbuttoned blouse.

And when the buxom divorcee needed a manly shoulder to cry on, well, there it was, along with the key to room 1204 at the Ramada Inn on Central Avenue. And the pretty secretary seethed with envy as they walked out arm in arm, *"Take my calls,"* he said. And she cried all afternoon, wishing she had never met him, until he stopped by that night to see what was wrong, and he took her on a ski trip to Colorado the next day, telling the not so pretty secretary, *"take my calls."*

But when the serious business of law beckoned, they were right on point, motioning and Your Honoring with the best of them. Winking, smiling, gesturing to the jury, having swallowed the Chesire cat. So when the jury awarded their client millions of dollars, they celebrated with all the lawyers in the building and all their wives. And the pretty secretary wasn't included in the celebration, and she sat at her desk, moving papers from left to right, maybe thinking she wasn't quite so pretty. *"Take my calls,"* he said.

24

"*You got people?*" the character in the movie asked the woman who sat at the bar crying over a miscarriage she had suffered that day. She looked up at him quizzically, holding back tears which refused to stay behind their barrier. "*Yeah, I got people.*"

I, myself, started off this life with many people. Over the years each of us added more people, and as they grew up and married, they added more and more people, maybe hundreds of them.

But little by little the numbers began to dwindle, as grandparents and parents, aunts and uncles, and sometimes even brothers passed away.

So today I look around me and see how few of us are left, and through the tears I can still say, "*Yeah, I got people.*"

25

In October, my friend Ed began his journey to Heaven, and I miss him. Oh, we weren't best friends in the sense of the word, but we were good friends. He was tall and distinguished looking. He represented all that was good about life. He was thoughtful, warm and caring, maybe a little cantankerous on occasion, but always a gentleman. He had a nice smile and when he laughed, his blue eyes twinkled. You could tell he loved his wife and was mystified by her independence. He had a brilliant mind, filled with amazing facts I knew just a little about, but I felt at ease just sitting around and listening to him talk. He enjoyed history and politics, German wine, visits to the Southwest, biscochitos and sunsets.

Yeah, my friend Ed has gone off to Heaven, but there's a little corner of Santa Fe where his spirit still hangs around.

26

Dustballs gathering at every corner, wispy dog hairs floating through the air, propelled by the push of air from forced heat. Dog feet steps imprinted in kaleidoscopic patterns on greasy sticky floors begging for a wash.

Windows cast a dull glaze over outside world, sunshine attempting to pierce the filtered haze. Wilted flowers sit in vases of stagnant water, long forgetting the representative event.

Dog leash hangs from nail, next to the paper valentine whose loving words have faded into now pink fibers. Walls hold scattered paintings, hung haphazardly at long intervals of white space, shiny green plastic laurel swings edgely, working its way to the floor knowing it will remain there forever.

Barely cracked open closets full of hardly and never-worn clothing, some with yellowed labels and orange sale tags hanging from tattered string. Dresser drawers full to capacity, underwear edges caught in corners. Jeweled box lonely alone on wooden shelf, tiny ballerina posed to begin its whirl, leg fixed in pirouette frozen in time.

Prayer books, *missalettes*, novenas and rosaries sit side by side next to empty candle glasses and scattered matchsticks. Indian head pennies mixed in with crumpled two-dollar bills in a flat silver bowl sitting on the dresser. Old perfume and baby powder, Ben-Gay tubes and rusted razors lay along the bathroom shelves, accompanied by unopened Avon bottle gifts, dental floss and Vaseline.

Rows of books with dog-eared pages line the shelves, propped by stacks of never-read magazines, an old rag doll stares pensively from the bottom shelf, and the Aunt Jemima marionette hangs on a nearby nail.

Grief waves over from top to bottom, unaware of hours ticking away. Red wine rides smoothly down, accompanied by fear of liking its taste too much.

Weeks and months of unopened mail, transferred from corner to corner of the counter tops, red notices blare past due stickers on originally white envelopes.

On the shower stall hang loosely, yesterday's and the day's before clothes, piles of twice used socks and underwear cover the corner floorscape. Toothpaste tube squeezed beyond recognition, white blue gel attempting escape through sides of the top. Mountains of dirty clothes piled high against more mountains of dirty clothes, towels resting in heaps against layers of Levi jeans and soiled t-shirts. Empty boxes of Tide and Clorox stand at attention, waiting to join the twice-used paper towels in the trash.

Television sets covered over with layers of infinite dust looking for yet more space to land on topped with wood and clay figures frozen in time, longing for a tender touch. Beds unmade with rumpled sheets and wrinkled comforters, pillows yellowed from sleepless nights of tossing heads. Pushed to the side lay books, dozens of books, with random colored papers peeking out between some pages, marking thoughts to return to already forgotten. Crumbs from necessary snacks scattered next to empty plates and bowls edged with dried milk and peanut butter. Pens and pencils of various colored inks and leads attached to unwritten thoughts on blank papers.

Boxes of letters bearing dates of long ago, 1966 expressing I miss yous; 1970s expressing I hate yous followed by crumpled up legal decrees divorcing one-time last forever till death do us part no longer lovers. Photos of happy children, arm in arm, she looking through the distance into future with eyes blurred by tears from past. Mega-memories reside inside heads of photo-occupants burned onto Polaroid paper. Chronicles of days gone by the wayside, hearts torn open by infidelity, brave souls holding chins up as knees buckle. Gaps in history not recorded, photos marred by chocolate fingerprints, holes poked with pencils hiding lies the camera never listened to.

Grandson's room sits quietly in repose, shades drawn to hide the time of day, day-old socks and used-once bath towels scattered haphazardly in every corner, school books peering out from side-laying backpack asking are you ever going to open me. Paper, pencils, quarters, pennies, nickels, lay floor-wise in no particular order next to crumpled watermelon gum wrappers and yellow paper scraps with hopeful phone numbers heaped high in anticipation of call me. Empty Coke cans wait patiently for transfer to recycle bin, there to join many of its kind.

Shrines aligned, shrine after shrine, spiritual mementos forming alliances, expressions of faith. Santo Nino dressed in dusty satin robes, sits majestically on broken feet with outstretched missing arms, tender eyes which look straight into souls. Dried dozens of once-red roses sit in glass vases intermingled with memories of those who gave the love bouquets. Yellowed photos of the loved ones, some framed some not, with prayer cards carrying news of when they went before us, looking out into rooms where unheard strains of music seep through cracks and fall on deafened ears. Waxed beaded flowers form the crown of Grandma's wedding veil housed in wooden case with glass door, sitting next to tin boxes parents' made while pounding tin on kitchen table wobbled over time. Saints and Madonnas adorn once-white walls, framed in ancient shiny metal stamped by hand speaking out with wisdom of century days and I could tell you stories of your culture if only you would listen.

Hallway winds around the house, passing double sinks filled to capacity with dishes tinged with scraps of ravioli, pizza, chicken McNuggets, chips and salsa, bordered by vestiges of rice and tofu uneaten by chopsticks. Tea bags and twice-licked lollypops stick together holding on for dear life. Newspapers from three yesterdays cover the tabletop, half-finished puzzles hold the secret of the magic words, boxes of chicken flavored dog treats sit idly by.

There's something else in my house, it is April 8, the tenth anniversary of my father's death. The cold dark studio flashes recognition as window shades snap curtly up, fluorescent lights cast their bluish glimmer on half-finished figures with unseeing eyes waiting for the sensuous scrape of sandpaper against their cold and wooden bodies. Finely sharpened tools amidst piles of curled up shavings, ideas floating through the air waiting to be caught by creative minds. Tables covered with clutter among which things are easily found unlike needles in a haystack. The lights go on, the hands sit at center stage, ready to perform their magic. Another day, another dollar.

27

By the time Rita was thirty, she'd been married twice, both marriages eventually going south. She wasn't *too* bad looking, even with the overly platinum colored hair she'd adopted after her first divorce a few years back, which didn't match her sallow complexion. She had an admirable wardrobe, though, peppered with hundreds of pairs of high-heeled and spike heeled shoes, each in their original box, some dating back to the 1950s. She was a little on the light side where common sense was concerned, always choosing to follow her heart, which mostly got her involved with the wrong kind of people. Maybe she was just searching for love in her own way, following the *zigs* in the road instead of the *zags*. Tired of living from paycheck to paycheck, she quit her job at the mall and decided to sell the house her mother willed to her and just move somewhere where she could get up late every day and sway with the music at night. Was that too much to ask? Rita loved to dance, and as you can see, she had the shoes for it. She could dance every dance from the Jitterbug to the Hustle, and she'd strut her stuff at every family wedding and celebration, and every other opportunity that presented itself. But times were changing. The only place you could find a guy who wasn't gay was in one of the local bars, and with all the rapes and stuff that happened in the last ten years, a girl just couldn't hang around a bar on a regular basis without asking for trouble. Besides, she wasn't getting any younger. Her kids were all grown and had moved away a long time ago. She had nothing against gays, her son just happened to be one, but she wanted to be married again, to be taken care of, secure, and happy, and not necessarily in that order.

One morning while pouring her eighth cup of coffee, having read all ten pages of the local newspaper, she was glancing through the classifieds for no particular reason. Maybe there was a flea market or garage sale somewhere nearby that day. Her eyes fell on an ad in the personals, which read something like: "Disabled man looking for live-in caretaker; non-drinker, non-smoker, must be willing to relocate. No experience necessary." *Shit*, she thought. *I can do this. How hard can it be? Keep the house clean and put him on the pot, change a few diapers and wipe a dribbling mouth, and I can smoke on my own time, and I don't drink much anyway.* After a ten minute phone call, she went to her closet, grabbed a suitcase and started throwing a few necessities into it. Early the next day she was winding her way up the Taos highway toward Colorado. Her final destination was a small town in the mountains, one of those you'd miss if you blinked your eyes. A little over two hours later, as she looked around, it looked to be little on the desolate side, with very few creature comforts: gas station, a Circle K and a video store, next to a Kentucky Fried Chicken clone. But, oh well, she was only checking it out. No commitment yet.

A few months later I saw her at the grocery store in town, where she was walking around with a basket filled to capacity. I asked her if she was feeding an army these days, and she gave me the lowdown on her recent move to Colorado. She was just here to pick up a few things before the wedding. Turns out she was going to marry this fellow she had started out just working for. All I could do was to congratulate her, after all, this could be the one she'd been looking for all her life. Attending the wedding was out of the question but I promised I would come up for a visit whenever I could pull away from my job, which didn't happen until six months later.

The first time I met Dallas he was in their living room, smoking a joint, sitting on the couch next to his wheelchair. He took full advantage of this form of prescribed medication. I don't doubt that he was in great pain from the injuries he suffered in the Gulf War. Rita casually mentioned the tank he was standing next to was hit by mortar fire and he was lucky to be alive. He was still a handsome man, with no outer scars visible other than legs which had grown reed thin, and uncooperative arms which struggled to maneuver the wheel chair he was confined to. Five minutes later we were sitting at the kitchen table, Rita pouring warm coffee and cream into a hard plastic cup with a straw, and he leaned over and asked me how I liked my sex. Momentarily taken aback I responded, *With two sugars, please*, thinking he was attempting to be funny. He was dead serious, and he followed with other crass comments. I didn't care for his bluntness, and I dodged the questions graciously. I wondered how many of his biting comments had cut holes right through Rita's heart. I guessed the monthly disability check, the diamond rings and the Platinum MasterCard to match her hair had a lot to do with it. Having grown tired of his deliberate digs, I decided to cut my visit short and head home. I looked over to say goodbye but he was busy lighting up the bong next to the couch, conveniently oblivious to my gesture. On the way out, Rita apologized, adding that she guessed he was just having a bad day, that most of the time he was civil. I guessed life with him was never a good day. There was no excuse for his conduct, disabled or not.

I never went back to visit, even though Rita came to town occasionally and we'd meet for drinks, but she always had to rush back to be home before sundown, otherwise there would be hell to pay. What kind of hell she never explained, but I could guess, from just looking at her bruised arms and occasional heavy makeup over one too puffy eye.

Dallas died a year or two after I saw him last, from complications brought on by pneumonia, and even though I was sorry, I wasn't compelled to go to the funeral. Hypocrite wasn't something I wanted to be. Her sister mentioned that the life insurance policies had left Rita quite comfortable and that she sold the house in Colorado and moved back to New Mexico. Although I haven't seen or heard from her in years, a friend of my brother's recently commented about a not half-bad looking older platinum blonde who hangs out at Cosmo's Bar in Albuquerque every Thursday night and dances up a storm all the way up to closing time.

28

It was a beautiful mid-summer day. Some time in the last twenty-four hours he lay down on the grassy knoll, rolled his Levi jacket up and placed it under his neck. There he laid, smoking Marlboros one after the other, until the blazing sun receded and the pumpkin orange moon rose slowly until it was right above him. Bright stars peppered the sky like sprinkles on a chocolate cupcake. He could almost reach up and pour himself a drink from the Big Dipper; maybe even sit inside it and rock himself to sleep.

He reached into his shirt pocket, crumpled the empty cigarette pack into a ball and tossed it over the fender into the bed of the army green truck. He unrolled his Levi jacket and pulled a bottle of pills out of the chest pocket, Haldol, I think they said. As he popped them one by one into his mouth and chased them down with the last Miller Lite out of the twelve pack, he chuckled at the sight of his cowboy boots, noticing one was black and one was brown.

The next day his brother found the body in the middle of that field, surrounded by purple wildflowers and tall olive green grass, a covey of quail strolled nonchalantly by. His mother showed up at my front door that evening, looked straight at me and said without flinching, you're the reason my son is dead. If you hadn't left him last month he'd still be alive.

Was I really the reason for his death? I think not. I knew him for only six months; they knew him for a lifetime. I surmised it was easier for them to lay the blame at my doorstep, than to look inside themselves to find the reason they buried him long before he was dead.

29

The little boy cowered in the corner of his room.

The lights were on but he sat in the darkness.

He covered his ears trying to block out the sounds coming from the hallway.

Years later he sings the blue songs, chases the blue ladies, and each day downs a handful of the blue pills, cowered in the corner of his room.

30

As the road winds its way toward home, I have mixed feelings. Did I find what I was looking for all these years, or was it always there? I was pedaling my bike as fast as I could, running toward myself. Somewhere along the way I saw my reflection off in the distance; but when I arrived at the fork in the road, I was gone.

My heart thumped with the realization of how close I actually came to finding me. But then one day the world changed. Jet engines roared and skyscrapers collapsed into rubble. Silent screams echoed through the dust. Suddenly I no longer felt safe, in this America, the land of the free.

Bogey women peered from jagged curtains covering closed windows, beckoning me to come closer, to look into the depths. But I turned and ran, feigning blindness. Who was there left to believe? The straight and narrow path had become a winding road leading to uncharted territory. Scarecrows sat ominously in fields of corn whose kernels baked in the late summer sun. All that was reliable disappeared from view. In its place came chaos, panic, fear, unrest and a hunger to find, regain or retain love. I was no longer wrapped in my blanket of security, my American flag.

My tears flowed behind me as I spun around in every direction; a great whirlpool of black dust swallowed everything in my midst. I was alone again. I wandered across the landscape, ever hopeful that a knight would come to my rescue. I had no magic slippers to transport me to the depths of my imagination; no Calgon baths to take me away. I was not the same. I will never be the same.

I gathered the charred remains of my life and gave them up to God; this Lord, this wizard, who had carried me on his back for so long.

31

My Tia asks a lot of questions. Oh yeah, she's ninety-three years old, and broke her hip last year, but she's still got a full set of working spark plugs. Sometimes it doesn't do any good to shush her because like a little kid she just talks louder. Like last week when we were at her Cousin Thelma's wake, she wanted to know why they weren't praying a rosary; my Auntie Zelda told her Thelma wasn't a Catholic anymore, ever since she took up with the Ah-ley-lu-liahs in the Valley.

"Well what do you mean," she said. "She was born Catholic and she died Catholic. You just don't go changing religions in the middle of the road. San Pedro's going to have some questions for her when she approaches that golden gate! What's she going to say, I changed my mind?"

"Shhh, Tia. You can't do nothing about it now. Just let her rest in peace."

"There's not going to be any peace for her if they don't at least have a priest at the funeral. Who's that chubby fellow with the mustache doing all the talking?"

"That's the *pastor*, I think that's what they call him."

"Oh, you mean the one who collects all the donations and then drives around in a new Cadillac?"

"Shhh, Tia. I'm sure he does his job."

"You mean stealing Catholics from the church? They used to come door to door, handing out pamphlets and wanting to come in and preach to us, but we never let them in! But they kept coming back, so the Padre gave us these little cards to paste on the front door saying this was a Catholic home and they just didn't pay attention. So every time we'd see them coming, everyone in the neighborhood would just not answer the door, except for Thelma, of course, who invited *everybody* in. You could sell her anything, that woman."

"Shhh, Tia. They're starting the eulogy."

And this stranger walked up and stood in front of the casket. He spoke of how generous Thelma had been, with her weekly donations and all that, and she even donated her car for them to sell at a raffle because her neighbor down the way always gave her a ride to services. After talking for a while the man then asked if anyone had anything to add. I looked around, and one or two people got up and alleluliahed a few times and then there was a quiet silence in the room. And you know what? My Tia stood up and started praying the rosary in a strong voice, *Santa Maria, Madre de Dios, ruega por nosotros pecadores...* and little by little everyone in the room followed. By the time of the last *Padre Nuestro*, everyone was in tears. I guess you can take the people away from the Church, but you can't take away their faith.

32

My *mamacita* prayed a million prayers in her lifetime, prayers which hurried up to *mi tata Dios* on paper wings, gently held together with the glue of hope, *esperanza*.

She prayed so we would.
She prayed so we wouldn't.
She prayed so we'd see.
She prayed so we'd hear.
She prayed so we'd believe.

She prayed that good things would come to us; that we would be protected; that we would be happy, loved and cared for. She prayed that our hurts would be small; our illnesses would be healed; and that our heavy hearts would be washed with tears of joy. She prayed that we would learn from our mistakes, our poor choices, and from our lapses in faith. She prayed that if we ever crashed and burned we would get up and walk away; that anger would never shred our hearts into pieces.

And many times she prayed we would each experience our fifteen minutes of fame, and if it was meant to be it would last longer. And she prayed, too, that at the end of our time on earth we would go softly into the night, without fear.

33

I grew up in a house without hallways. No wide halls to walk down holding your arms out like an angel whose wings whisked against the walls dislodging tiny fragments of dust. No hallways that separated rooms which could be closed off by a wooden door, where private thoughts could be thought and clutter could be hidden from view. No rooms which could be darkened by closed doors and drawn curtains, blocking off any hint of daylight. No rooms in which a tired or lonely body could sleep until forever. In our house, we were welcome in every room. We walked from room to room without the need of hallways, rooms which had no doors, only archways to separate them. Archways which would pass the light from room to room, with added light coming from transparent panels hidden under heavy curtains pulled together only at night.

You couldn't run and hide in our house, except maybe in the bathroom which had a door, or my parents' living room/bedroom, which also had a door. But neither of these rooms were available full time for hiding or crying. I wonder if the hallways would have made a difference in separating us from each other. Would we have been less inclined to wonder what was wrong if we couldn't see the fearful looks or the red eyes; if we couldn't hear the painful sighs, the nighttime sobs or early morning laughter? Our house was built without an architect, without a blueprint, with only a drawing in the dirt made with a stick. It was a rectangular adobe box with four rooms of almost equal size, with rounded archways in between to keep life flowing through from room to room. Yes, we had no hallways to run down holding our arms out like angel wings; but we had a house where life lived.

34

Emerging from a burning house
He said goodbye
With anguish in his eyes
But she looked away
His insides tied in knots
His eyes fixed on her face
But she wouldn't budge
Her mind made up
His hand moved swiftly
Across the canvas
Layers of paint covered her face.
The love burned hot
As she faded from his touch.
He slept the deep sleep of the dead
With nightmarish ghouls dancing on his soul
She was gone
She had placed her memory in a Gucci bag
And sped away
When he awoke, only ashes remained
The angel said to him
As he quenched the embers with his tears
You can breathe now.

35

*C*andles
Illuminate and
reflect
tears
cried over fallen objects.
Las velas
illumbran
la fé
de la génte
en sus altares.

36

My cousin Pita and I spend a lot of time with Auntie Sara and Uncle Robert, since we're their only living relatives, and they're both getting up in years. Mostly I help Auntie clean her house and cook a meal once in a while, and sit and watch Sex and the City with Uncle Robert, since he says he likes to keep up with the younger generation. Mostly I think he likes to imagine himself young and virile once again, reliving the days when he used to be quite a Romeo. Auntie Sara just ignores him when he sees a pretty girl at the J. C. Penney store in the mall and tries to act all handsome and everything. *"Honestly, Viejo,"* she says. *"You were staring so hard you almost walked into the window of Blockbusters Video!"*

Today, Cousin Pita has decided she's going to take Auntie Sara to Albuquerque, to some big lecture they're having at the University so they can get some culture. Pita is studying to be a nurse's aide and she believes if she attends all kinds of programs it will help her understand the patients better. But she's not sure what kind of presentation this is, something about the "Virginia Monologues," and one of her co-workers recommended that she go listen to it, so she bought two tickets, thinking I was going with her. I had already promised Uncle Robert I would take him over to the Jiffy Lube to get his car greased, and you know that Uncle's schedule takes priority over anything else that's going on. So Auntie is getting dragged along to sit through this presentation and Uncle Robert needs to know what it's all about, since he might just want to tag along himself.

"I don't know, Viejo, Pita didn't say much other than she had gotten two tickets and thought it might be interesting. Some big movie stars are going to talk about Virginia somebody or other."

"Well," he says, "knowing how much of a rabble rouser Pita

can be, it's probably political. Maybe there's a Senator from Virginia who's going to be there?"

"I don't think so, Viejo, she didn't say it was political. Just a bunch of movie stars talking about this Virginia. Maybe she's a movie star, too. You know how they're always having a benefit for every worthy cause that comes up. Anyway, we'll be back in time for dinner."

So Pita and Auntie take off, and while they're on the road to Albuquerque, they talk about stopping for a quick bite to eat in Bernalillo, since they still have plenty of time, and besides the lottery is up to eighty million and they might as well stop off at the pueblo gas station and get a few tickets. You never know.

When they arrive at the stadium, they're both surprised by the number of people standing in line to get in. Thousands of women, and not one single man. *This Virginia must be a very popular woman*, thinks Auntie. By the time everybody sits down and all the introductions are made, the program gets under way. Auntie keeps turning up her hearing aid because the acoustics in the place seem to be very poor and she has trouble hearing what the women on the stage are talking about. Every so often the place breaks into laughter, and she looks over at Pita, whose cheeks seem to be very red. *Must be the heat, since it's kind of a warm day.* Auntie quits fiddling with her hearing aid and decides to just leave it off. She doesn't understand much of what they're saying, anyhow, and it will soon be over and they can go back home.

On the drive back to Santa Fe, the women don't do much talking. Pita tells Auntie she's sorry for dragging her off to such a crowded place and hopes she wasn't embarrassed by the whole thing. Auntie tells her not to worry, since it was all above her head anyway, but thought it was very nice that so many women have so much respect for this Virginia that they could talk so much about her. What she couldn't figure out is why did some of them holler at the top of their lungs and cry out in agony.

That evening, I heard Auntie trying to explain to her Viejo what the whole afternoon was about. "I don't know, Viejo, there were a whole bunch of women there. The place was so full that they were even standing in the aisles. And the women on stage were not only talking about this Virginia, but they also keep talking about their Chinas."

"What do you mean, Vieja. Was this lady from China?"

"I don't think so, but every one of them kept talking about 'my China' and how much love they had for it and how sorry they were that they had ever mistreated it or been embarrassed by it. And everybody in the place kept clapping and hollering, I love my China, until it was finally over. And then this lady next to me started talking about how wonderful that women could talk about their private parts and how times had changed. I realized what she meant and I think I turned red as a beet!"

"Dios Mio, vieja! Next time Pita decides to take you to another one of her wild goose things, you better make sure what it is. I'm sure glad I didn't go with you because after listening for a while they would have had to call it the Angina Monologues because I sure would have had a heart attack listening to all those women talking about their coochies!

37

Mother frequently related stories and offered warnings to keep us on the right side of the tracks during Lent, and at the time, we trusted their veracity. She recalled that she and her sister, Sally, while living in *Ojo de la Vaca*, were drawn to the music coming from an old dance hall on a long-ago, dark, Good Friday evening. The sun had barely set as they departed from the house, telling *Mama Ines* they were going next door to play with their cousins. Fifteen minutes later, shivering with excitement, they crept up to the windows of the dance hall and looked in to see what was unfolding within. According to my mother, *"It was just a one-room dance hall. It was filled with thick smoke, so much that it hung like a curtain from the ceiling down. Los musicos were sitting in old wood chairs on a stage raised about a foot from the ground. First they played a soft valse, and then a quick polka. We tapped our feet and swayed our hips to the music as we stood on the mound of dirt near the window. Sally and I sure wanted to get in there and dance, but Mama would have skinned us alive."*

I found it comforting that her generation had pretty much the same rules for Lent and Good Friday that we did. It assured me there was something to this religion. She continued with the story, *"Everybody was all dressed up, you'd have thought it was Easter Sunday. The women were todas perfumadas, with lipstick and rouged cheeks. They wore high-heeled shoes and nylons, and their jewelry rattled as they danced. The music got louder and louder, and everybody was drinking and dancing. You could hear the laughter right above the music."* Mom stopped for a minute, got up and checked the bread baking in the oven, taking a few minutes to beat an egg yolk and spread it quickly over the top crust before putting it back in the oven.

"Then", she continued, *"a tall, handsome man stepped into the*

room. *Oh, he was good looking! He had dark wavy hair which formed small curls at his neck, and these piercing dark eyes, that sparkled anytime light hit them. He must have walked right by us, but we didn't see him. All the ladies swooned as he took them out, one by one, to the center of the dance floor, spinning and twirling them to the enchanting rhythms of the music. Sally and I watched, thinking we should go in and join the festivities, and we had almost talked ourselves into it, but we sure knew better."*

Rosalie and I listened intently as Mom described the way the women's dresses spun as they twirled around to the tempo of the music. She became animated as we waited in anticipation for the next part. *"What happened then, Mom,"* we asked in unison.

"Well, this man kept dancing with all the women, and their viejos were sitting at the bar, glaring at them, while they sputtered and giggled in delight, coyly fluttering their eyelashes. Suddenly, one of the women let out an ear-piercing scream! Holding her hand over her mouth in horror, she pointed to the mysterious stranger's feet! As they all looked down, they saw his hooves, and then a pointed tail slowly emerged from under his jacket!"

We sat at the edge of our chairs, minds racing to imagine what would happen next. And Mother continued with the story. *"In the middle of the screaming, everyone headed for the door but they couldn't open it. It was shut tight. One of the men ran over and kicked it open, and the smoke tumbled out the door in waves as if propelled by a strong wind. Sally and I turned and ran home and never looked back. We couldn't imagine what would have happened if we'd gone in there. Dios Mio! When we got home, Mama said we looked like we had seen a ghost. We said nothing and jumped under the covers, clothes and all!"*

While she had us captivated, Mother added, *"The moral to the story was that if you're going to do something forbidden on Good Friday, el Diablo won't be too far behind."* Of course, we were always careful not to break any of the Lenten rules, since Mother repeated the story every year, embellishing it each time with a subtle twist.

—Excerpt from *Tortilla Chronicles: Growing up in Santa Fe*

38

Angie wouldn't ever talk to anybody. She wore a warm winter coat everywhere she went, even in the summer. She liked warm wooly coats, but they made her look like a big bear. Kids at school made fun of her, but she just turned and walked away. She went through every year of her life wearing a big coat, buying another one as the last one wore out or she outgrew it. It didn't matter what the color was, as long as it was warm. But was she cold? I never asked. I assumed maybe she just needed to have that that protection around her. To keep her from feeling. To keep her insulated from the taunts and barbs on the playground. To keep her safe. I tried to be her friend and she looked at me through big green eyes; with surprised eyes. I didn't need another friend, but I would have been a good friend. But she wasn't buying it, and she turned and walked away, without a word. She just wrapped herself around her heart until she grew older and her heart gave out. Maybe she hadn't kept it warm enough.

39

Growing up in Santa Fe in a neighborhood in the South Capitol area, everyone protected children from harm. Even walking down Galisteo Street toward town was a little easier knowing I had three big brothers, and they all had friends who treated us like we were family. It wasn't so much that the street was lined with bogeymen, but every so often someone would intimidate or frighten us. Anytime that happened and Bobby was nearby, he would make it a point to let them know who they were messing with, and the offender would sheepishly say he meant no harm. He was always our personal protector because he knew so many people. I had always been afraid of shadows but Bobby's presence in my life made me feel just a little bit safer.

Born in 1934, by the time my brother Bobby was nine, he slipped out of the house and wandered around town every night with his friend Robert *Satch* Trujillo. He was noticeably different from the rest of us, he was a nonconformist bent on breaking the rules. All sorts of handy items followed him home—roller skates, bicycles and food. At Christmas time when Santa Claus visited the Plaza, an event sponsored by the 20-30 Rifle Club, children and teens stood in line to receive small paper bags filled with hard candy, a pat on the shoulder, a Merry Christmas, and a ho-ho-ho. Bobby would stand in line and then exchange jackets with one of his friends and get in line again, arriving home carrying a large cloth bag popping at the seams with Christmas goodies. This also happened on Halloween, he would traverse up and down the east side neighborhoods and bring home pillowcases full of every kind of candy imaginable. Easter egg hunts kept us in boiled eggs and chocolate rabbits for weeks.

Bobby was thoughtful, caring and compassionate, but even so, he was always in trouble. His police record began when he was ten.

The first time the police knocked at the door with Bobby in tow, my parents thought he was tucked safely in bed, like the rest of us. He dressed differently, stayed out late, had problems in school. He spoke differently, with a heavier Spanish accent, and didn't switch back and forth from Spanish to English like we did. My parents experienced ongoing conflicts with him and they seemed to argue more about him. Throughout his life, Bobby always believed he was the black sheep of the family.

Years later, he confided in me that he was always treated differently, that he believed none of us liked him, especially our parents. I thought he was exaggerating, since over the years he managed to garner more attention than all of us combined. I believe my parents were completely befuddled by this dark-haired, dark-eyed young man, who reminded me of a story I read about a gypsy child wandering out in the desert. The concept of "tough love" did not exist in those days, just discipline meted out by parents who were trying to hold a family together in the face of great odds—too little pay for too much work, too little food for too many mouths. When one of the wheels squeaked far too often, the inclination was to silence it.

Bobby squeaked a lot, but in a way that must have grated against the very core of my parents' being. In his case, they never knew where they had gone wrong, or even if they had. The harder they tried to rein him in, the worse the situation became. After a while, anything and everything he did was wrong. With a broad smile on his face, he brought home dessert from the bakery where he worked, but his absences from school overshadowed this gesture. A toy brought lovingly home for one of us would raise the question, "From where did you steal it?" I don't believe Bobby ever considered my parents' viewpoint, or imagined that they might have been right.

To the rest of us, that meant not making any unnecessary waves. There were small secrets about each other we kept as children that were never mentioned to our parents, for fear of being singled out for punishment. For instance, the bicycle and skates Bobby brought home one day immediately became items one of the neighbor kids might have forgotten to take home. The last thing we wanted was to be responsible for someone else's whipping. You never knew when something we considered minor could be blown out of proportion by a wrong frame of mind—better to not mention it at all. I know I was willing to do anything to shift the focus away from Bobby, as I'm sure my brothers and sisters were.

In a journal late in life, Bobby wrote:

"It is hard to make people believe that at the age of twelve I was making $150.00 a night. After picking an armful of roses and carnations from the huge mansion of the Greer's, then I'd walk over to the state capitol grounds, and pick a whole bunch of yellow daisies and chrysanthemums. I'd put three or four flowers together with a nice ribbon, which I pilfered from the five & dime. And here I go downtown to Emil's Nightclub or La Taverna, loaded with fifteen or twenty bouquets of flowers." These he would sell for one or two dollars, depending on how much alcohol the guy had consumed.

"If the guy didn't buy the bouquet, it would embarrass the hell out of him because I would continue to stand there, all innocent looking, with a smile on my face as though I knew something about him he didn't want known. The girl would usually coax him to get the flowers for her. Sometimes he would slam the money on the table, grab the flowers and tell me to get out. If too much of a fuss was raised, the bartender would grab me by the neck and push me towards the street."

Business continued at a brisk pace during that summer. Homeowners around Santa Fe's east side continued to wake up each morning to find their prized irises and gladioli had been picked during the night, and there wasn't a rose in sight. In addition, the ribbon inventory at the five and dime continued to get smaller, particularly when Bobby was forced to take a partner into the business. One day, he was approached by Big Julio, who informed him of the two choices he had. First, Bobby could stop doing business all together and Julio would take over the territory; or, second, Bobby could make Big Julio a partner and they could share in the profits. Bobby chose the latter, and business continued as usual.

"Business was really good while it lasted," he recalled. "We were up to twenty or thirty bouquets a night. My part was the selling and Julio's was producing. By midnight we had them all sold or the bars were empty. We'd split the money, and I'd go home for the usual ass-kicking."

Somewhere in the back of Bobby's mind, he must have hoped my parents would look upon his newly found wealth as something positive. But they didn't.

"I never could understand how I was so good at making money but no matter how good it was, there was an ass-kicking when I got home, there was a definite lack of communication. It was hard to explain all the money in my pocket, so my dad just thought I was stealing it."

Everything was going all right in school, with Bobby attending as often as he was inclined, and the flower business continued to boom. That's when the proverbial shit hit the fan, as one night he and Julio prepared to walk into Emil's night club, bouquets of flowers in hand, and two police officers greeted them at the door. It was the beginning of a downward spiral in the life of a teenager who considered his only wrongdoing to be his desire to earn a little money.

"This was my first encounter with the police and with the corruption that would lead many a good kid to reform school, prison, drugs and alcohol; and then to die because of a system that made you a rebel," he said.

The first night in jail was a hellish adventure. Because they were juveniles, he and his friend Julio were escorted to the women's quarters, and the sound of the iron doors closing was a sound that would stay with him a long time. There was one mattress, one blanket, and one toilet. He could hear crying and yelling all night long. The winos brought in during the night raised all kinds of hell with the police, and they could hear combative inmates being pushed, shoved and beaten until they hit the ground. "For breakfast," he recalled, "they gave us some S.O.S,(shit on a shingle), two slices of bread and thin coffee, none of which I could eat 'cause I was so worried about what was going to happen when I got home." About nine o'clock, Bobby was taken downstairs to be questioned about breaking curfew, stealing flowers and selling them in the bars. In the view of the police he had committed a crime, although Bobby didn't see it that way. It was just a way to earn a commodity sorely lacking in his life...money. Fortunately, he was sent home with just a warning, which was little comfort, knowing there was going to be hell to pay at home, since he had been out all night, and in jail to boot.

After a short stint working at the bowling alley downtown, Bobby's next job came while attending Harrington Junior High, cleaning the small animal cages at Santa Fe Laboratories. He was responsible for feeding the rabbits, guinea pigs and rats, and after a few weeks on the job he concocted another money-making scheme: he could sell these small rodents to his classmates. Life was good until two white mice slipped out of his jacket in English class, causing the teacher and the girls to scream in unison.

He was expelled from Harrington the next day and sent to Harvey Junior High, a school already noted for its many rebellious students. It was there he would fall into another world where his moneymaking abilities allowed him to make friends easily.

It wasn't long before he was arrested after a gang fight with a group from Los Alamos. Bobby recalled the incident and the feelings that ran through him as he faced the prospect of losing his freedom. "It was the first time I cried. I was doing my best, and what I did wrong was to protect myself," he said. "I was going to have to appear before a judge, to explain what was happening, and I figured I had less chance there than a snowball in hell." By the time he was sixteen, he was sentenced to spend the rest of his teen years, until age twenty-one, at the reform school in Springer, New Mexico, with his sentence to begin in sixty days. Springer is a small village about 135 miles northeast of Santa Fe and had a population of less than one thousand at that time. The facility was a corrections and detention center built for juvenile offenders. Bobby was declared an incorrigible truant for consistently ditching school. At the hearing, Judge Scarborough gave my parents a severe tongue-lashing, blaming them for each incident, saying Bobby lacked discipline at home. They didn't understand why the judge would treat them with such disrespect, blaming them for everything Bobby got into, but they took the blame gracefully as the judge handed down his harsh reprimand. During the ensuing months, Dad drank more and more often, and Bobby stayed out all the more. It was a battle of wills, and we weren't sure who was going to win. Discipline had little effect on Bobby: he was a free spirit. Every time Dad took his belt off to whip him, Bobby never cried, and the whipping continued, and he still wouldn't cry. I recall Rosalie, Jimmy and I watching nervously from the living room window, trying to hold back the tears. I saw in my Dad's eyes the frustration he felt as Bobby refused to buckle under the belt. When it was over, Bobby came into the room to comfort us, saying "Hey, what are you little *vatos* crying for. Don't worry, it's okay." The next day he'd bring us a slightly used toy he had stumbled over on his way home.

Eventually, it came time to take him to Springer to start serving his sentence. My parents' hearts broke as they watched the deputy place handcuffs on Bobby's wrists, put him in a van and drive off. In tears, I stood watching from the porch, waving goodbye and wondering if I would ever see my brother again.

"I sat in the back seat of the van, with Cousin Raymond, who was to be one of my few trusted friends, and a guy they called 'Green Eyes'," Bobby told me. "I was the only one handcuffed, so the other two could move around. You'd have thought I was Al Capone. It was a long hundred and thirty miles."

Arriving at Springer, he observed some of the boys playing baseball or walking around the grounds. As he looked around, he saw the areas were fenced and fairly clean. Green Eyes' voice brought him back to the moment. "You know, Carnal, we better hope somebody we know is in charge. If there's more guys from 'Burque, they control everything that goes on; if there's more guys from Santa, then they have control. No *te agüites*, don't get all worried," he cautioned.

Fortunately, Bobby soon discovered at that particular time Santa Fe had the most "guests," many of whom he was acquainted with. According to the judge's ruling, he was to be placed in the fourteen-to-sixteen- year-old area, but instead he went into what was referred to as the "Big Building" that housed the hard-core older inmates. His room was on the third floor, and he was the youngest person in the building.

"The first night was the worst. You could hear sobbing and praying all over the place. As many as five guys would rush towards a bed, throw a blanket over the guy, and proceed to beat him up. Everyone had ice picks and home-made knives for protection, but they had to be hidden from the guards. I couldn't wait to get me one."

Life at this boys' reform school was such that Bobby had to draw from his innermost strengths simply to survive. His days were filled with intense intimidation coupled with harsh punishment for even the most minor offenses and severe beatings for major offenses. He developed self-discipline, knowing he was going to be there for some time. He dutifully made his bed, did his laundry, and worked on the alfalfa detail, and listened carefully when the cafeteria workers told them what foods to avoid, since sometimes mess hall boys deliberately doctored the food with dirt, semen and sawdust.

When an inmate was disciplined, he was placed in the center of the room with everyone instructed to form a large circle around him. The guard lowered the inmate's pants and proceeded to whip him slowly and severely with a leather strap. "I learned early on if I was in line for discipline," he recalled, "that I should start bawling like a baby after the first contact with the strap. This would show I had learned my lesson. The guard would stop whipping a lot sooner, because it was hard to hit a target who was pissing and moaning."

He continued, "All this time I only had one thing in mind, and that was to get out. Every couple of nights something would happen that would completely unnerve me, a senseless beating carried too far, or inmates attacking each other after hours."

"We looked forward to weekends, though. On Saturdays, we were given two sacks of Bull Durham tobacco and two boxes of matches, and let out to play ball, run, or do whatever you wanted to do. In the afternoons we were all marched about four miles into the town of Springer to the Zia Theater, which was the best thing that happened. Since we were all dressed in Army clothes, it must have been quite a sight, marching like a miniature platoon. On these occasions, we were harassed by the townspeople, but all we could do was throw fingers at them. The guards enjoyed having us on display. Of course, the locals always stared because they recognized the military uniform and the shaved head. Many of them looked at us like we were really bad criminals and held on to their kids like we were going to eat them."

Recalling his first few months at Springer, he said, "For me the first months were fine. Every so often, the folks would come to visit and take me downtown to eat at the diner. I looked forward to seeing them, even though it seemed like my dad was uncomfortable being there. I'm sure he was, but it was sure nice to get away from that place for a few hours.

"Sitting in my room looking out at the other buildings, it seemed to me they could have sent most of the occupants of the Big Building to war, cause it had its killers, rapists, butchers, psychos, and each one ready to kill if it came down to it. These were hard-core criminals, and not too many of them were even close to being twenty-one, but still too young to be sentenced to the Pen. They would have made a hell of a fighting army."

After nine months of his sentence, he was released and assigned to Mr. Kilkenny, his probation officer in Santa Fe. Bobby was given a suit (which he said was probably stolen from somebody else) and a bus ticket to Santa Fe. "Getting home was quite a thrill; just going to the park you had the walk of the Chuco, the respect of the guys, and sometimes the choice of the girls. After arriving home, at first came the lectures, and a couple of dollars here and there. I started going out with a redheaded cheerleader from Harvey Junior High, where I had to go to school, and I sure found out what I was missing. It wasn't too long before most of the guys who had been with me at Springer were out on the streets, so I started hanging out with them."

Sitting at the kitchen table one afternoon, I listened as Dad encouraged Bobby to change his life for the better to work toward putting the past behind him. In essence, finish school, get a job, and grow up. It appeared as though the past year had an impact on him, and he returned to school with determination. But it wasn't long before a downward cycle began. He participated often in gang fights, beatings and rumbles, and continued hanging out with other teens released from Springer.

"First of all, under the terms of my probation, I couldn't hang out with these guys, so that was the first time I broke the law. Then we stole a car and drove to Española. About ten people piled in, everyone drinking wine and beer and just having a ball. We got the car back to Santa Fe, stripped it and sold all the parts," he recalled.

The downward spiral continued. Walking into the gym bathroom at Harvey Junior High, he was shoved against the wall and severely beaten by a football player. "I went home looking more dead than alive, and the first thing that was asked was 'Who did you hurt?' I didn't go to school for two days, and when I did, everyone laughed and snickered at me."

He continued, "So that night I went down to Alto Street and talked to the guys about what happened. The next day I took twenty guys to the school and we kicked the shit out of every football player we could find. I knew they would report me to the juvenile authorities, so I quit going home."

Eventually returning home, he learned the truant officer had already been there and a court appearance had been scheduled. At the hearing, the judge was unaware of anything other than a probation violation for missing school, but Mr. Aragón, the truant officer who had it out for him, brought up the recent altercation and the judge sent Bobby back to Springer.

This time it wasn't the same. The Albuquerque inmates now outnumbered all the others, thirty to fourteen, and he was the new kid on the block. "After getting my ass kicked a couple of times, I started carrying small balloons filled with air and chili powder in my pocket. If someone attacked me, I would bust one on their forehead and the chili would get all over their eyes and burn like hell. It would be days before you could wash that stuff out."

To escape from Springer involved consideration of a number of factors: "To the north is Raton, all desert, and you can be seen for miles; to the west is Santa Fe, but the Sangre de Cristo Mountains have to be crossed; to the south is Las Vegas, all rolling hills, and to the east, barren hills. There was no way out unless you stole a car. I always said that if the earth ever needed an enema, Springer is where they would stick it in!" Springer was considered the bowels of the earth by the inmates, and escape was not only difficult but risky. But that didn't mean Bobby wasn't going to try.

Early on in his stay he witnessed events that made him more determined than ever to escape. A young black inmate was severely beaten by a guard for his refusal to use the wrapper on a roll of toilet paper to clean himself, throwing it in the trash instead. With his pants still down, the guard dragged the boy over to the dining table and proceeded to whip him with a belt until he fell to the ground. A few days later a young inmate named Ace was caught with a few bottles of booze in his possession. The guards ordered everyone to form a circle around him, and after this was done, he was told to lower his pants and the guards commenced to whip him with a laundry belt. "After over fifty lashes, Ace still refused to cry and it angered the guard even more. The guard continued the whipping, moving up to his neck and back. Everyone in the room was begging Ace to cry so the guard would give up, but he just looked straight ahead. When another guard finally stopped the beating, Ace turned around and smiled, and then just slid down the wall and died on the floor." Bobby was greatly affected by this. "I had never seen anyone die, especially from a beating that wasn't even fair. They just kept hitting him until he couldn't take anymore. I don't think I'll ever forget seeing that single teardrop fall from his eyes as they closed. Then they told his parents he fell on a rock climbing trip."

Whenever my parents visited him, they took along our "care packages" consisting of magazines, cookies, candy and chewing gum, which he eagerly looked forward to. His fellow inmates created their own liquid refreshment. "A few of them would steal alcohol from the leather shop and cut it down with orange juice. They strained it through four slices of bread and filled jars with their own brand of reform-school moonshine. When the guards discovered the liquor, the offenders were disciplined first with the strap and then by having their heads shaved.

Of course the guards confiscated the moonshine and stuck it in their own lockers."

Tired of the beatings he endured from time to time, Bobby decided to get even with some of the meaner inmates. "One time we cut our moonshine with prune juice and left a big jug of it out where it could be seen. About twelve guys drank a good slug out of the jug. In about twenty minutes, everyone had the runs and there weren't enough bathrooms or toilet paper to accommodate them all."

A few months into his sentence, Bobby met "Flat Top" on the alfalfa stacking crew, and together they began to hatch an escape plan. They spent one morning stacking alfalfa bales in the barn, leaving a tunnel down the center. They cut some nails in half and kept the sharp end to spread in the parking lot to flatten the tires of the guard's vehicles. For several weeks, they collected apples, oranges, raisins, candy bars and cigarettes, provisions enough to last about two days in the tunnel.

When the guards were in the cafeteria for dinner, the boys plan was to take off running across the grounds to freedom. One cloudy night, they waited near the boiler room for the trustee to come in and shovel coal. Seizing the opportunity, they flew out the door, intending to knock both the guard and the trustee down. "But the old bastard held on to the door," he said, "and Flat Top couldn't push him out, so I ran out and hit both of them with a flying tackle and we all fell. We got up and ran towards the river. We stopped behind the shops to catch a breath and heard the old man blowing his whistle. We ran into the barn just as it was getting dark and dove through the hay bales into the tunnel. We flattened the first few feet so it would look like there were only hay bales."

Tired and out of breath, and in pitch black about twenty feet into the tunnel, the only sound to be heard was the fast beating of their hearts. Bobby stretched out and heard a strange sound near his ear, probably a mouse or rat, he thought. "Flat Top, light a match! Nobody will see it anyway."

Flat Top lit the match and held it out in front towards Bobby's head. "Right in our path to freedom was a damned rattlesnake. Somehow Flat Top scurried behind me and I'll never know how. I think the tunnel was only about eighteen inches wide. He started screaming and tossing hay in every direction, and when we finally cleared the entrance, there were five guards standing over us."

In his haste to escape the rattler, Flat Top dropped the ignited match and set the hay bales on fire. In a few minutes, the entire barn went up in flames. After the fire was extinguished, the boys were directed out into the yard, where all the inmates hung out from their windows, hooting and laughing. As they neared the main building, they could feel the tension rising. The guards told them they knew what punishment to expect, and to take it like men.

"Right away, Mr. Caldwell opened the cupboard and got the strap. I thought I was going to get the worst part, but he grabbed Flat Top first and gave him a good beating, including kicking him in the balls. Then it was my turn, and he hit me a dozen times and I fell down and scurried under a table. Everybody in the building was laughing, so I came out and he finished the job with his hands."

For the next few days, their meals consisted of sliced bread and water, but under the table they were handed more than enough food to survive. Having endured the beating and the head-shaving that followed, it would be a long time before Bobby was ready to escape again, but not too long.

It took six months to develop an escape plan, and one night, he and two other inmates decided the time was ripe. Hastily forming a dummy for their beds, (the characters in *Escape from Alcatraz* must have borrowed their plan many years later), the three snuck out of the building, ran to the outer perimeter of the grounds where they cut the barbed wire fence and ran toward the town of Springer. Lalo, one of the trio, found a car to hot-wire, and made sure it had gas, and they headed toward Santa Fe, jumping up and down, hollering and whooping that they'd made it out of there.

Fifty miles out, the car sputtered to a stop, and as they pushed it off the road, Bobby and the other boy teamed up and began walking through the fields next to the highway toward Santa Fe and Lalo headed north toward Colorado. Fearful of catching a ride with someone who might turn out to be the police, they walked through fields and gullies and over rocky hills. At some point they decided to head south, in the direction of Mexico, knowing the authorities would be looking for them in Santa Fe. Several more days passed as they hitchhiked toward anticipated freedom. They imagined arriving in Juárez to begin new lives, emerging after a few years as successful bounty hunters or the like. Their anticipation would be short lived.

Bobby recalled the event: "We rode across the border crossing just outside of El Paso and into Juárez in an old farmer's truck, surrounded by chickens and pigs. We were happy and laughing. Man, we were free at last! We didn't care if all we had to eat was scraps from the garbage cans outside the restaurants...we were free! And that's all that counted."

After about a week, the adventure ended quite abruptly. The two hungry, disheveled teenagers were arrested by the Mexican police as vagrants, taken to jail and thrown into separate cells. After what seemed like an eternity, Bobby befriended one of the guards, who let him call home. "I made the collect call and waited. The first connection failed and I almost cried. The operator couldn't understand our telephone prefix, 'Yucca' and I didn't know what the numbers for it were. The Mexican operator kept asking, 'Yooca, Senor?' On the third or fourth try, the phone started to ring. My heart was beating like crazy and my forehead was sopping wet. One of my sisters sleepily answered the phone and I just said, 'Get Dad.' I was sure he was going to raise hell and hang up, but he didn't. I told him everything I could and he said he would try to get me home. I could barely hold the tears back when he said 'God bless you' and hung up."

The shock waves created by a collect call from Juárez in the middle of the night turned our somewhat peaceful world in Santa Fe upside down. Mom continued praying, and Dad was upset, but at least we knew Bobby was still alive. Fortunately he was released from the Mexican jail two months later after Senator Dennis Chávez from New Mexico and an attorney negotiated with the Mexican authorities. Compared to the horrible conditions he had endured in the Mexican jail, fighting flies, cockroaches and rancid food, returning to Springer would probably seem like a return to paradise. Dirty and disheveled, and ten pounds lighter, he returned to Santa Fe. The senator and attorney met with the judge and arranged for Bobby to be put on probation. He would not be required to return to Springer.

It wasn't long before Bobby donned his slicked-back Elvis haircut and pegged khaki pants and assimilated back into life in Santa Fe as though he'd never been gone. Pachucos had a certain gait, each step a slow and deliberate shuffle, hands in pockets. They were renegades. Their side hair was slicked back with pomade, and the top hair was styled into a curly pouf. I watched with fascination as Bobby nailed a horseshoe-shaped metal tap onto the heel of his shoe and several smaller ones to the front sole. You could hear his footsteps clearly as he walked on the concrete sidewalk next to our driveway, and visibly annoying my father as he walked through the house.

Every so often there was a *rumble* between different gang factions around Santa Fe. A member from a Manhattan Street gang took a strong dislike to Bobby and was looking for a chance to kick his ass. One night a dance was held after a basketball game at St. Mike's, and during the intermission, everyone was milling around outside, laughing, talking and smoking.

"I looked up and saw this guy coming at me. Before I had a chance to take my jacket off, the guy lunged for me and I felt a cold, sharp piece of metal pushed into my chest. Oh, I was hurting bad, and the pain made me dizzy. I couldn't talk, or think, or anything. I fell to the ground and the next thing I remember I was laying in a bed at St. Vincent's Hospital, blood all over the place, and then I passed out again," he recalled. The hospital staff refused to administer any medical aid to him until my parents were contacted. I remember the telephone rang in the middle of the night, startling me out of a deep sleep. Rosalie and I slept right next to the phone, and she reached over to answer it. She sat up and screamed to Mom that Bobby had been hurt and they wanted them at the hospital right away. My parents dressed quickly and took off for the hospital. Jimmy came home a few minutes later and we told him what happened. He grabbed his keys and went out the door and we could hear the loud noise of his car's mufflers all the way to the end of the street. When my parents arrived at the hospital, they were told that Bobby suffered a bayonet wound an inch away from his heart and that he was clinging to life. After my parents signed the papers, the orderly wheeled him into surgery, still unconscious. My mother said it was a miracle that a few days after surgery, Bobby slowly began to recover. The police came to interrogate him, but he refused to reveal the name of his attacker.

He explained, "It wasn't even a fair fight. The guy who knifed me was under investigation for the murder of his father, but I wasn't going to tell them anything. Right off the bat they decided to bring charges against me. I don't know for what...standing there and being stabbed?"

As the district attorney began to gather evidence to prosecute Bobby, my parents again turned to Senator Chávez for help. They couldn't endure the pain of seeing him taken to the reform school at Springer again. Through a mutual agreement between the district attorney and my parents, Bobby enlisted in the Army in late 1952. He returned home a few years later with an honorable discharge; he married, and fathered several children, but like a magnet, crime was always sticking to the soles of his shoes. In 1958 he and five friends walked into the downtown Sears-Roebuck store, and each walked out with five pairs of pants. Arrested outside the door, the officer promised if they paid restitution to Sears, they would just be charged with petty larceny. But it didn't work out that way. By May of 1959 Bobby was declared a habitual criminal by the court and a hearing date was set for sometime in the future.

I recall the day he unexpectedly walked into Judge David Chávez's law office where I worked for Attorney Joe Guthmann. (Judge Chávez was Senator Chávez's brother). Bobby must have considered me his last chance. He told me that a hearing was scheduled for one o'clock that day and that he had no attorney to represent him. With his shoulders slumped forward, he revealed that the district attorney wanted to send him to the state prison for twenty five years. He was visibly shaken and scared. I think he must have realized this was serious business, no six-month stint at the reform school. His demeanor reflected no arrogance, no belligerence. I went into the adjoining office and spoke with Judge Chávez and filled him in on the details of the impending hearing. He expressed concern that Bobby had waited so long to see an attorney. Compassionate man that he was, he put his arm around Bobby's shoulders and told him he would make no promise, but he would do his best.

At the hearing, Chávez was successful in having Bobby's sentence reduced to one to ten years at the New Mexico State Penitentiary, although I had hoped it would be less. It's hard to imagine what my brother went through, knowing all the wrongs he had committed in his life now cost him his freedom. Some years later, he said, "You know, I could tell you stories about prison that would make your head spin. I saw stuff that would make a grown man want to crawl away and hide under a blanket and never come out. I tell you, I could write a book about my experiences." I wish he had. After serving part of his sentence, he was released from prison on good behavior. He eventually found a job in Phoenix but returned to Santa Fe sometime later. In the ensuing years he remarried and became a hardworking and law abiding citizen.

In recent years he had begun to follow the footsteps of my parents and was creating beautiful items handcrafted out of tin. Over the years his health began to deteriorate, due in part to years of drug and alcohol abuse; coupled with severe rheumatoid arthritis that required additional drugs to ease his pain. Much to our dismay, he died on Veterans' Day in 1997 at the age of sixty-four.

As I sit on the back deck of my house, I notice my yard is basking in the splendor of spring. It is a lazy Santa Fe day. The lawn chair wraps around me like my mother's arms. I am thinking about the dead. Not all the dead—just my brother. All these years later I still don't understand why he died. God didn't have to take him. He could have taken some *borracho* off the street or a pothead, a *marijuano*. I feel such anguish that he died, I'm sorry that I never said *I love you*, assuming he probably knew. My thoughts went back to the 1950's, remembering how foolish I thought he was, him thinking he looked a little bit like Elvis Presley as he ran his fingers through his hair. I was sorry he had so much trouble feeling loved. One time when he drank so much that he asked me to take him to a place where he could dry out, but when we got there he changed his mind. He screamed in anguish that he couldn't stop, *maybe another time,* and the sorrow in his eyes was too much to bear. I knew then how a mother felt. What had happened to him; how did we let him get to this point? I wasn't strong enough to budge him, and I had no words to console him because his ears had closed when he was a child. He had forgotten how to listen. I put my arms around him and just said "Okay, whatever you want." And we came home, sixty miles in deafening silence. He was lost in a liquid land that offered momentary relief to his pain.

Throughout the years I felt a particular closeness to Bobby. He so strongly believed he was the black sheep of the family that it seemed that he went out of his way to prove it. Years later, we had an intense discussion about his life and the emotional pain he had obviously endured. Drugs and alcohol had never eased this pain. He carried a lifetime of scars that couldn't be erased. He seemed to long for an apology that life had dealt him such a rotten hand. My father was a stubborn man and believed he had treated Bobby on the same level as the rest of us; unfortunately, there was never a resolution to the sadness they each felt toward each other. I'd like to believe that perhaps now they're together in some little corner of heaven, talking things over.

40

Waldo sat in the lawyer's office, glancing first at his watch and then at the framed certificates from Georgetown University hanging on the wall above the massive mahogany bookcases. He shifted his weight to get comfortable in the too small armchair. Not that he was heavy or anything, but yeah, he had let himself go a little. At least he had all his hair, albeit it was almost completely gray, but women his age still considered him to be somewhat handsome. Ben Rodriguez, on the other hand, was every father's favorite son. Not only had he graduated with honors from his law school, but he had married his childhood sweetheart, who was also an attorney and president of the local bar association. They owned a horse ranch in a nearby community and a six bedroom house in the upper eastside. He was a family friend and distant cousin, fifth or sixth in a long line of lawyers. As he cradled the phone between his neck and ear, he shuffled thick stacks of paper from left to right. Every so often he looked up at Waldo and made a motion with his hands about the woman on the other end going on and on. Waldo thought to himself that the meter was probably running on his clock and not hers. Ben finally hung up the phone, clasped his hands and looked directly at Waldo.

"Okay, Waldo. Refresh my memory...the last time we met you said you were interested in filing a lawsuit against your Uncle Raymond. What's going on here?"

Waldo proceeded to relate the story, trying to include as much information as he thought was relevant.

"Well, about twenty years ago when my father was still alive, we were sitting around the kitchen table having a few beers. Uncle Raymond came in and sat down and joined the conversation. We were talking about my sister's mother-in-law who had this huge ranch in

Cerrillos just south of Santa Fe, and after she died there was a big old fight over her estate. Apparently the old woman had left everything to the ranch hands and nothing to her son and grandson. So the family was embroiled in a huge lawsuit. Anyway, I looked over at Uncle Raymond and asked him how come grandma and grandpa's estate had never been probated. He told me he thought that fell under the category of none of your business. He stormed out the door and went directly to Uncle Eloy's house to tell him what I had said. Well, the next day, Uncle Eloy came over and literally ripped my dad a new one! He said it was none of my business and he should teach his sons a little respect. Dad told him I was an adult and I could ask whatever questions I had and, besides, if they weren't always so damned secretive about everything they did, people wouldn't be wondering what they were up to. Anyway, the brothers ended up not talking to dad for about seven years and it really hurt him. I felt bad that an innocent question had caused such a rift in the family. At some point my Uncle Eloy started getting sick and had to be hospitalized a couple of times for stomach problems. Compassionate man that Dad was, he would send my mother down the street to Eloy's house to take him a meal here and there and to make sure he was all right. Eventually he too began to go over to visit Eloy, but they never talked about what had happened. I think Raymond eventually started coming around, figuring all was forgiven since Dad had started visiting Eloy regularly.

Six months or so elapsed, and one day Uncle Raymond and Uncle Eloy came to my folks' house and sat down at the kitchen table and chitchatted for a while. After a few minutes of small talk, Uncle Ray handed my dad a check. Dad looked at it for a few minutes and asked what it was for. Uncle Raymond told him it was a down payment for what they owed him as his part of their folks' estate.

"You see," Waldo continued, "for as many years as I can remember, Uncle Raymond built houses and every time he needed money, Grandma would sign some sort of papers on the house so he could borrow enough money from the bank to do the construction. Anyway, at one point, one of the brothers talked Grandma and Grandpa into putting the house in Uncle Eloy's name so they wouldn't have to pay taxes since he had a Veteran's exemption.

"So when Grandma died, of course the house would have gone to Grandpa since they were both on the original deed, but it was still in Eloy's name so they didn't have to do anything. Grandpa never recovered after Grandma died. One day I stopped by to say hello, and Uncle Raymond said to not bother him because he was asleep. Well, I waited until Raymond left and went in anyway. Grandpa could barely talk, unlike the booming voice we used to hear when he hollered at us to climb down from the damned apricot tree. He was skin and bones—half the size he used to be—and couldn't have weighed more than eighty pounds. There was a bottle of whiskey and a big shot glass on the table next to his bed. He said he couldn't remember the last time he ate and could I give him a little water and maybe some food. I went into the kitchen and there was nothing in the refrigerator but an old loaf of bread and some butter. I warmed up the bread and spread some butter over it and sat on the edge of the bed propping Grandpa up with one hand and giving him little pieces of bread with the other. Uncle Raymond stormed into the room and asked what the hell I was doing and that Grandpa was too sick to be eating, and he grabbed the plate out of my hand, sending the bread flying onto the floor. He told me to get the hell out and proceeded to pour a full glass of whiskey and had Grandpa sip it until it was all gone. Anyway, a couple of weeks later, Grandpa died. After a month or two passed, they rented the house to a young couple who stayed there for about five years and it's pretty much been rented since. Uncle Eloy continued to live in the small house in the back where he had lived for the past forty years. My dad never knew what happened to the rent money, but he knew better than to ask. The third brother, Uncle Gerald, was a pretty peaceful kind of guy and he never asked questions either. By the way, he also received a check that day, the brothers telling him it was a down payment of his share of the estate.

"So everyone went about their business. My dad figured that eventually they would either come with another check or they would sit down and figure out how much each brother was owed and make some sort of settlement. He commented since they had kept all the rent money for the past seven or eight years, they had probably considered that part of their share. About two years ago, Uncle Eloy got himself in a jam. He was a character, that guy. Since he was pretty much homebound except for a weekly trip down to the liquor store to buy a couple of bottles of red wine and some groceries or to the Carmelite Monastery where he would take the nuns a pot of pinto beans he had cooked, he watched a lot of television. And you know how they have all those telemarketing programs day and night where everything sounds like a good deal... anyway, he started buying things right and left and putting them on his MasterCard. Every time I went over to visit him, he had a freezer full of frozen steaks from some company in Omaha, and a few dozen boxes of salted nuts, chocolate candy bars and a whole bunch of records, CDs and DVDs. He had almost every gadget advertised in magazines and on television, including some kind of metal bar which would extend out so he could get things from the upper levels of the cabinets. Not only that, every so often he would point out a new washing machine or some other appliance he had just replaced. This must have gone on for a long time, and I knew that the only money he had coming in was a small disability check from the VA and an equally small Social Security check.

"Sometime during those years, my dad began having health problems and he eventually passed away. In the months before he died, we had talked about different things, including what the brothers had promised to pay him as his share. He said to make sure they took care of it. Anyway, I figured that being family, eventually Uncle Raymond would approach me to take care of the matter, but he never did. My dad strongly believed in a man's honor, so I too figured they would do the right thing. So I just waited.

"One of my cousins called me one day and asked me if I knew the financial mess Uncle Eloy had gotten himself into and that the bank was getting ready to take some sort of action on his credit card debt. I went over to talk to Uncle Eloy and he told me that he got a little confused and thought everything was coming out of his checking account, that he was using a debit card, and since his checking account always looked okay when he got the statement, he didn't worry about it. Well all of a sudden he gets a letter from an attorney demanding that he pay over $18,000 in credit card debt to the bank. He almost had a heart attack and didn't know what he was going to do. My cousin and I thought the solution was simple. He could get a loan on his little house and pay them back. The payment wouldn't be much more than one of his checks. Besides, he was still getting rent money and that would also cover the payment. We assured him we would help him arrange what ever he needed to do, and he seemed relieved. Well, in comes Uncle Eloy and starts telling him how he's going to land out on the street and have nothing left; that the bank is going to take away his house and Grandma's house and everything else he owns and that he won't be able to borrow any money, and who's going to take him in, he's going to be homeless with nothing but the clothes on his back. I stopped by a few days later to see if Uncle Eloy wanted to go talk to the people at the bank and he said no, he had changed his mind. His brother was going to give him the money to clear up all his bills, and all he had to do was sign a paper giving Raymond title to both houses. That way he would be able to live there until he died, and still collect the rent money, and besides, he knew his brother's word was good, so he was going over to the attorney's office that afternoon to sign the papers. Boy, I could see he was getting screwed! I tried to tell him how much both houses were worth, and that was way over $450,000 in the current market, and he could even borrow a home equity loan on one of the houses to pay that credit card bill off. He didn't have to sign his life away. But Raymond had convinced him his way was the right way, the only way, and Uncle Eloy was sure he was doing what was best for him. I don't think he was capable of making a decision like that, considering he was taking a lot of medicine and still drinking a couple of glasses of wine very day."

"I see," interjected the attorney. "What's the status of the property now?"

"Wait, it gets better," continued Waldo. Uncle Eloy seemed to be getting stronger every day; he wasn't even drinking his daily glasses of wine anymore. Sure, he was still on a walker and his legs would swell up every so often, but he was getting back to his old self, smiling and laughing when something was funny and keeping himself clean shaven. Raymond's daughter Hannah used to come by every couple of weeks to balance his checkbook and make sure he wasn't getting out of control again, but other than that, neither of them came by much, after all, they had the title to both houses, what else did they need? My cousins across the street from Eloy's house were spending a lot of time with their aging parents, Uncle Gerald and his wife, who also had health problems. They always had a soft spot for Uncle Eloy and the fact that he never had children, so they would go over every day to take him food, clean his house, bathe him, and everything else he needed. I went over a couple of times to clean the yard and loaded all the trash in my truck, and my sister brought him food as often as she could. Anyway, all of a sudden I hear Uncle Eloy is in the hospital and when I go see him, I find out Hannah has somehow appointed herself his power of attorney, or as she puts it, 'caretaker', and she's giving me this bullshit that he's gone crazy, completely lost his mind, and they're going to have to put him in a home somewhere, because *oh-my-God*, she's so exhausted from taking care of him for the last few months, and she wrings her hands and cries a few alligator tears while I'm there. So after they leave, I'm in there talking to Uncle Eloy, and he asks me to get him out of there, but I know he's too weak to walk. My cousin Jillian comes in, and she tells me she knows he's not crazy, he was all right until he started taking the new medicines prescribed by the doctor a few weeks before. So she went out to the lobby and called her husband to look it up on the internet and sure enough, if you mixed this medicine with alcohol, it could have some really weird effects, like hallucinating and instability. Back in the hospital, she tells the nurse about it and the nurse says, *are you the 'caretaker'*? And Jillian tells her no, but my husband works for the District Attorney's Office and if you don't tell the doctor to have this checked out, I'm sure I can arrange for it to be done another way. As it turned out, she was right about the medicine, so he seemed to get better after a few days. When it came time for him to be released, though, Uncle Raymond and Hannah convinced the doctor that since he was going to need full time care once he got home, there was no way they could take care of him, and besides, they really couldn't afford to pay someone to come in every day and

Medicare would pay for the nursing home until he got well. So, they got their wish. Uncle Eloy was declared indigent, and transported to probably the worst nursing home in the area, but by far the cheapest. The ceilings were so low you could reach up and touch them, and there was always a really foul smell in there, like maybe someone had died a while back and they didn't notice. After a few days, Raymond went over to the house and had the utilities turned off since he figured there was no point in paying for them. *Damn!* They couldn't have been more than twenty-five dollars a month!

"So time passes and Uncle Eloy starts getting better. His nephews and nieces visit him frequently and little by little his spirits start to pick up. When I went to see him, he was in a dark and depressing little ten by ten room that he shared with another patient, and his bed was in a corner with barely enough room for a small table. The drawer contained everything he had to his name: An empty wallet, his statue of the Blessed Virgin, half a Hershey bar, and his rosary. He told me that all he had left in this life was his faith. He had no home to go to, no television set or radio, and none of his personal things. Even his two heavy winter jackets and a pair of good boots had been stolen out of the meager closet in his room, so all he had in there was a pair of worn pants on a hanger. He didn't even know if his cat was still alive or had starved to death. I knew all my assurances fell on deaf ears, but I tried anyway; we all felt so sorry for him and the blows he had been dealt. He always thought he would spend the rest of his life in his little house, watching a little television and listening to Mexican music on the radio. Some time passed and my cousins started picking him up on weekends and taking him to Uncle Gerald's house, wheelchair and all, where they would feed him breakfast and lunch, spend a lot of time visiting with him, and then taking him back by dinnertime. At first everything went okay, but then one time he decided he didn't ever want to go back to the nursing home again. He said he wanted to die in his own house. It took them a lot of time to convince him that he needed to go back, after all they knew there weren't any utilities in the house, and besides that, they knew they would be in a world of trouble if they didn't take him back to the home. Well, they finally got him back and waited a month or so before they started bringing him back to their house again. They brought him for Thanksgiving, on his birthday, and then for Christmas and many times in between. It was sad to watch him looking out across the street to his house. Sometimes you could see tears welling in his eyes and we knew how difficult it must be for him, but he tried hard to stay positive. After the first of the year, I ran into one of my cousins at the grocery store, and she told me that Uncle Eloy had taken a fall in the nursing home and that he was back in the hospital. Well, this time we could see the writing on the wall. We all doubted whether he would make it, and even though he tried to rally a couple of times, I think he finally decided he couldn't bear the thought of going back to that empty, hollow space he had been relegated to. He died in the middle of the night. There was a small rosary service attended by family and a few old friends, the funeral pretty cut and dry. We all gathered outside the church to form a small caravan to the cemetery, but Uncle Eloy said the mass was all there was, and we needn't go to the cemetery, as there was going to be nothing there. They didn't even give him the military burial he was entitled to with the twenty-one gun salute and the American flag being handed to the family. For all we know they could have tossed the ashes in the back of a garbage truck. We couldn't believe it, but Uncle Eloy and Hannah were in charge of everything, and she was still spewing phony tears all over the place, still talking about how exhausted she was taking care of him all those many months!

"Back to your question. As far as I know, Uncle Raymond had hired a high-power attorney to draw up all the papers when he originally had Eloy sign them. He wanted to make sure there were no loopholes and that nobody would be able to dispute them. In fact, I recall he may have told one of my cousins that, but I don't remember when or where. In the meantime, I had several discussions with my cousins about pursuing what I felt was rightfully my father's inheritance, and although they agreed, their father was still alive, although up in age, and he didn't want to die knowing that there was a family dispute brewing, so he asked them to honor his request and leave it alone. So they did. A while back, Uncle Gerald died quite suddenly, leaving Uncle Raymond as the remaining brother.

"So now that Uncle Gerald was gone, Raymond decided he could start clearing out Uncle Eloy's house, and I mean clearing it out. He must have felt guilty doing it before, because he knew Uncle Gerald used to sit by the window looking out at Grandma's house where he had grown up. They backed up a big old flatbed trailer and just started dumping everything on it, clothes, food, knickknacks and everything else. It was as though it didn't matter that many of these things were precious to Uncle Eloy, but at least they didn't throw all of the religious statues on top of the pile. A week later they gave the tenant at Grandma's house notice, and started clearing that house out also. The tenant said they had only given him a week's notice, and that they were getting ready to list the house for sale. So that's why I'm here. I thought maybe we could file some kind of lawsuit to stop Uncle Raymond from selling the house or making him pay what was rightfully owed to my dad and to Uncle Gerald for that matter. You see, from what little I know about the law, I thought each of the brothers would have been entitled to a one-fourth share of the estate had it ever been probated. I can assure you that Grandpa probably never knew he had signed the house away for the last time. Anyway, about a month after Grandpa died, Raymond signed the house over to Eloy and that's how it stayed all that time until last year. It wasn't enough for that greedy bastard to screw my father out of his rightful inheritance, but he ultimately screwed Uncle Gerald and even Uncle Eloy out of theirs, even though Eloy had been a willing ally to Raymond for so many years, he really got it in the end, and Raymond did it completely without conscience."

"Well, here's the thing, my son," offered Ben Rodriguez. "You know how sticky family disputes can get. The laws have changed so much in the last fifty years that I'm pretty doubtful we would be successful in trying to salvage anything out of this mess. First of all, so much time has elapsed. You should have done something while your father was still alive. Yes, I know, you believed your Uncle would do the honorable thing, but you can't forget that money does strange things to people.

"And secondly, you have no proof that there was ever anything more than a verbal agreement between these two to pay your father and uncle an amount other than what they paid initially."

"But," Waldo interrupted, the fact that the two brothers were paid at the same time, and that the children were aware of the transaction, wouldn't that be enough?"

"Well," continued Ben, "that's good and well, but it's really your word against his. He can say that the twelve hundred they paid each of the brothers was their share of what the property was actually worth at the time. He can also say that the brothers agreed, even if it was just a drop in the bucket. No judge in his right mind is going to hear a case where everything is based on hearsay, that is, your dad said this and your uncle said that. Without any more proof than that, we'd be fools to pursue this. But I will say this. I think that by the time they get ready to sell the property, they are definitely going to have to file a suit to quiet the title. I don't think anyone will buy a property where the title has gone back and forth so many times. The buyer would want to be assured everything is clear and he's not going to run into problems down the road. And who knows if the signatures on the deeds are even legitimate. You know how easy it would have been to sign a paper with the mother's name to hurry up the process; after all, they had done it several times in the past. We could have a handwriting expert examine the various deeds, but I'm not sure where that would get us. It's something to consider. So, give me a couple of weeks to do some further checking and see what we can come up with. I can't give you any hope at all at this time. Honor and a man's word don't seem to mean as much as they did in your father's time. As much as we'd like to believe that Raymond is going to be forthcoming with any payment at all, it's unlikely, based on the fact that money and greed seem to be what drives him. And from what I understand, his daughter Hannah would like nothing better than to raze the two houses and build a couple of condos there. I'm surprised they're considering selling the property at all at this point. The last time I passed through the neighborhood, it looked pretty run down to me. Well, let's set something up and I'll see you in a couple of weeks. Meanwhile, leave my receptionist a substantial deposit so we can get started."

"You need to understand that this isn't about the money,"

added Waldo. "There are a couple of issues and they involve respect and honor."

"Yes, I understand, Waldo. But history is full of family confrontations, and in the end, the one holding the biggest wallet usually wins. It sounds like Raymond has the upper hand on this one. So leave that deposit with the receptionist and I'll get back to you."

It wasn't too long before there was a real estate sign in front of the property, along with printed flyers giving the particulars on both houses, playing up how much potential there was, how someone could combine them either to make one large house, or use the smaller one as a rental. After all, the east side of the city was a very desirable location, and this property was right in the middle. At the end of the month Waldo drove by the old neighborhood and saw that there was a "sold" sign attached to the top of the other one. He wondered why there had been no word from Ben Rodriguez since their last meeting, so that afternoon he made it a point to call him.

"Well," Ben started. "I've been meaning to call you, but you know how things go. I've been in court for the past two weeks on a murder case, so I haven't had one free moment to tend to things. I did have a meeting with your Uncle's attorney, and they're pretty adamant that there's been no wrongdoing with regards to the property. He says that according to Raymond, your father was paid off a long time ago, and that was that. As I mentioned to you before, I'm pretty sure they're going to have to clear that title somehow, but then again who knows what they're thinking. The attorney said as far as he was concerned, the title appeared to be fairly clear, having passed from the parents to one of the sons, and then from one son to the other, so he's not anticipating any difficulty when the sale is concluded. *Mira*, Waldo. Your family and I go way back, but I think you're just going to have to let this one go. I can keep looking into it, but I don't know if it's going to do any good. This can set you back many thousands of dollars, and I know you can't afford what it might ultimately cost. So, my son, I don't know what to tell you."

Waldo couldn't believe his ears. Surely there was something that would keep Raymond from selling off the property and keeping all the profits; money he wasn't entitled to keep. When he went to talk to the priest last week, Father told him he needed to let it go; to move on. Justice would have to take place in Heaven. Waldo told the priest that wasn't the point. Nobody would know about it there. The priest admonished him to be careful about letting his emotions run out of control. After all, if Raymond didn't have the capacity to see what he was doing was morally wrong, it was doubtful that a lawsuit was going to convince him. Family, property and money have never been a good mix, and this was no exception. Raymond feels he is entitled to the property and the money, and there seemed to be very little anyone could do to convince him otherwise.

That afternoon, Waldo stopped by his grandparents' house to see what changes were being made. He walked into the kitchen where a workman was cleaning a spot of tar on the floor with turpentine and a rag and not having very much success at it. Waldo suggested he might use gasoline instead and the man went out to his truck and came back in with a plastic gas can, poured a little bit on the rag and proceeded to slowly remove the spot. He thanked Waldo for the suggestion, looked at his watch and said his day was about done. Waldo walked out the door with him and went home.

The shrill sound of fire engines in the middle of the night cut through the cold air as the vehicles noisily wound through the narrow streets. The loud ring of the phone next to Waldo's bed woke him abruptly from a deep sleep. "Huh...what??" he answered. The caller on the other line was his cousin, David, who told him Grandma's house was burning down. The whole neighborhood was standing outside watching the flames reach the top of the old apricot tree, which stood several feet above the roof of the house. Waldo jumped in his Toyota truck and drove the few blocks to the old neighborhood. He had to park about a block away, and walked up the incline in the cold chill of the late winter night. He could feel the heat from the fire as he approached. It appeared nothing was going to save the house as the fire had burned for many hours inside before anyone noticed. David had gotten up to turn the television set off in the living room and reached up to draw the curtains when he saw flames shooting out of the windows of the second story across the street. By the time the fire engines arrived, the fire had almost completely consumed the remainder of the house. Hours later, as they stood outside surveying the damage, Uncle Raymond screeched into the driveway, demanding that the firemen tell him what had happened. The fire chief explained to him that apparently there were some gasoline soaked rags left in the kitchen next to the gas heater which must have ignited the fire, at least that's what the preliminary findings were. The house was burned to a crisp, with only a few of the walls standing. It had been too late.

As Waldo walked down the hill, the thought came to him that maybe justice wouldn't have to wait. Raymond had just received his earthly dose. It was going to take him months and a lot of money to rebuild the house, particularly since he had cancelled the homeowner's insurance policy about a year ago when he was cutting down on expenses, and the pending sale would surely be cancelled. Waldo decided he wasn't going to worry about it anymore. As he looked heavenward, he knew it was time to let it go. His dad would have wanted that.

41

I tell you, life was good in the 1950s. A person could be ten or twenty pounds overweight and nobody cared. Very few home bathrooms had a scale, and if you had a driver's license, it said you weighed one hundred pounds whether you did or not. Every female was an All-American Girl, completely natural, except for an occasional wad of Kleenex stuffed into a too large bra cup. Heavy makeup was reserved for special occasions, like maybe graduation or the prom, but for every day, a little bit of face powder and a touch of lipstick sufficed.

Long before Dolly Parton's hooters hit the big screen, the boys in our high school had their own mega-momma. Marilou was probably a few pounds leaning to the side of tubby by today's standards, but nobody noticed. She was also one leaf short of a branch, but nobody noticed that either. Nobody knew the color of her eyes, or the color of her hair, or even if she was two or more feet tall. What they did notice was her fully loaded pair of forty-fives, aptly describing her heavenly hooters, which were every male teenager's delight to behold. Hers were the things that dreams were made of. These ormufulous glands walked through the door a full minute before the rest of her did, the coral-hued angora sweater screaming in agony, stretched to its maximum capacity. She casually looked over her shoulder and fluttered her inch long eyelashes, while guys squirmed in pure delight, their imaginations running amok at the endless possibilities. Pretty much all the girls were envious of the attention Marilou received all during High School, since most of us were flat as pancakes, our small mounds barely making a difference next to her rocky mountains. It seemed that every potential boyfriend was living and reliving his fantasy every time she walked into a room, and their heads couldn't help but turn a full three hundred and sixty degrees each time she walked by.

So, as I stood in front of the mirror in my bathroom, why all of a sudden was I thinking about Marilou and her legendary chest? Small town as this was, none of us had run into her for years, and assumed she'd married some prince charming and moved to his castle in Paris. But surely we would find out at the fiftieth reunion of our high school graduation coming up this summer. As I read the invitation, I wasn't surprised that the people in charge of the reunion were the same ones who had been in charge of every event during high school. They were the members of the Honor Society, the Class Presidents, the teachers' pets, and anyone else of note. Class rosters in hand, I was sure they judiciously scoured every telephone book in the state searching for addresses of graduates from that year, and successfully managed to find almost everyone, including a few who had died and graduated to their eternal rest. No matter how much the city had grown these past twenty years, many families retained their roots here, some still living in the family home, most of which, incidentally, had increased two-hundred-fold in value since then.

To say some of us were hesitant to attend the upcoming reunion would be putting it mildly. High school years were difficult for those of us who were wardrobe and fashion challenged. In many large families in our neighborhood, shoes and underwear had to last an extraordinarily long time before being replaced. We prayed to avoid a dreaded hospital visit which would expose our tattered under things and holey socks unnecessarily. A few of us who had remained friends over the years had little intention of showing our cellulite and wrinkles and still meager chests at the welcoming dinner which would in all probability consist of a buffet with baked chicken, prime rib, potatoes, rice, German chocolate cake and fruity Jell-O. We dreaded being a captive audience, forced to hear more than we wanted to know about successful doctors, lawyers and Indian chiefs gleaned from the lists of graduates, conveniently bypassing the Go-Go Girls, Strippers and clerks at Wal-Mart, if perchance there happened to be any. But come-on! This was the fiftieth, and probably the final reunion for most. We were probably lucky we had made it this far and were still standing upright.

Jolene, Darlene and I met for lunch at least once a month. The three of us had been inseparable since high school, where we were known as the Three Musketeers. On this particular day, we were sitting at our usual table near the window at the Koffee Kafe, drinking our third round of decaf. We discussed the pros and cons of attending the upcoming reunion. As a normal course of conversation, our topics usually waxed and waned when we tired of any serious chatter, but believe me, we were shushed more than once as we erupted into gales of laughter remembering how Mr. Putnam's pants used to ride up into his crack as he wrote our assignments on the blackboard. No matter how hard he tried to untuck them by pulling and wiggling, his pants stayed firmly crotched in place. Jolene added that it was because he had no ass to begin with so his pants had nothing to hold up. The Coach was a different story, however, as his muscular frame popped right out of his clothes. It would have been a pleasure to zip his fly. But I digress. The question up for discussion was whether or not we were going to attend the reunion; and if so, how much preparation was it going to require pulling it off without embarrassing ourselves. We each added our two cents about why we did or didn't want to go. I offered that I didn't feel I had anything in common with the majority of the students then, and I doubted if that had changed much over the years. Jolene felt inadequate around people with vocabularies and boobs bigger than hers; and Darlene just couldn't wait to see who was still skinny as a rail and who now weighed four hundred pounds. God knows she herself had tried every diet in every women's magazine, finally coming to terms that a few pounds or more might not really make a difference. We still looked pretty good for our years, the middle aged spread having spread a little farther than we would have liked, but nothing so serious that it couldn't be fixed by a month of laying off the breakfast bagel and cream cheese and the occasional drive by the take-out window at Kentucky Fried Chicken.

One of us (Jolene) was still married to her high school sweetheart, and two of us (Darlene and me) had made the trip down the altar too many times to mention and were now facing old age and retirement without a mate to share the trip. But there was still hope. After all, if by now my old boyfriend Howard hadn't lost all his hair or gained two hundred pounds, I might take him up on his last invitation to meet for dinner, which was written inside the Christmas card he sent last year, long after his third divorce. He seemed to have done pretty well for himself over the years. His grandfather left him a cattle ranch about a hundred miles from town, and although he spent a lot of time out on the range, he still cleaned up pretty well, and besides, I've always had a soft spot for a man in Levis and cowboy boots. Darlene had been fluttering her eyelashes at the UPS man for about a month now, and that might just bear fruit; and if not, she was thinking of asking my brother Jerry, although I seriously doubted he was ready to drag his dancing shoes out of the closet where they'd hung out since cheek-to-cheek dancing went the way of the line dance.

Darlene and I are still debating whether or not we even want to go. After all, we didn't attend the previous four reunions, and it was doubtful too many of the grads would be able (or even alive) to attend a sixtieth; so maybe, just maybe, we might want to go check this one out. Unless they had a few Botox treatments or plastic surgery, most everyone wouldn't look like their high school photo anyway.

The three of us had survived middle age without incident, except for those extra fifteen pounds on our behinds I mentioned earlier, which were also packed on courtesy of the $7.95 lunch special at Maria's Mexican Kitchen every Wednesday as far back as I can remember. But there was still enough time to get rid of most of it, maybe by also cutting down on the potato chips, Cokes and such, New Year's resolutions which managed to have already gone astray. Lent was coming up and that was always a good occasion to give up a few things. Darlene said they might still sell girdles in the lingerie section at J.C. Penney, and she was going home to look through their catalog just in case, but Jolene said these days it was easier to find a garter belt than a girdle. She recalled that on one of those television shows you could buy some kind of panty hose that would shrink not only your ass but your ankles too, so she was going to see if she still had the phone number written on a tablet in her bedroom. As long as it didn't fit like a wet suit, it might just work. So, okay, it appears we had made the decision to go, and of course, Jolene was all for it, but she was wondering if maybe she shouldn't ask Herman if he might want to tag along, to which we both shouted a resounding "No!" Besides, we argued, he wouldn't know anybody there, and after a while he'd probably start whining about going home, a bout of flatulence having started shortly after eating half a dozen or so cheese taquitos in the bar. We left the coffee house in good spirits, the critical question now being what we would wear and how much it would cover.

It wasn't long before we started seeing posters around town asking "*Did you Graduate in 1959?*" There was a number you could call to sign up for the fiftieth reunion if you hadn't yet received a letter.

At the next lunch meeting between the salsa and the margaritas, our conversation turned to tidbits of gossip tastier than the fajitas we had ordered. The local Mayor's reelection campaign was in full swing. Jutting out at every curve in the road were bright orange octagonal signs saying "STOP! You can only GO if you vote for Arthur Chacon." The signs were the brainchild of Chacon's campaign manager, attorney Barney Sedillo, who was intent on making sure the reelection was in the bag. After all, Sedillo had been promised the City Attorney's job. But as bedpans and politics go, little did he know the election was about to take a sharp left turn.

On the other side of town, tongues were wagging and ears were burning as the local gossip mills went into full production. A certain incident had the making of a scandal like no other this small town had seen in a while. Perhaps a short history lesson is in order here. Arthur Chacon had been the mayor for about six years, chosen when the previous mayor's car drove off the road into the canyon after an all-night strip poker game at the Blue Rooster Bar. Chacon's last election was less than the landslide victories of previous campaigns, and the current race was neck to neck, so Barney was doing everything he could to make sure the Mayor was going to get all the votes he could generate. He spent a lot of time at the Senior Citizen's Center, promising free tokens to the casino up north if they voted for his candidate (and you know how some of those seniors just love to sit in front of the poker machines.)

About three years ago, Loretta Munoz moved back to town after working in Washington DC, as a secretary to the senior congressman from New Mexico. After a month of perfecting her tan at the spa, it wasn't too long before she was out looking for a job. The pickings were appearing pretty slim unless she wanted to make a hundred mile trip every day to work at the nuclear power plant. So when she heard the mayor's secretary was going to be out for six months on maternity leave, she decided to apply for the job, hoping it would be a stepping stone to bigger and better things. Mayor Chacon was more than happy to replace his secretary, Rosa, as she was something of a busybody. She kept his wife informed of every move he made, suspicious or not.

As I mentioned, Loretta still maintained her youthful appearance, a fact of which she was very proud. She looked much younger than her fifty years, never having had children or husbands to drag her down, so she spent a lot of time and money keeping herself in shape. It wasn't long before the two started a bit of hanky-panky, taking long lunches and traveling together to meetings in nearby communities. The mayor's wife was oblivious to everything around her, except her three-story house and her dog, since Rosa hadn't been calling her to give a daily report. As her bi-monthly visit to see her mother in California came around, her husband kissed her on the forehead and had his driver whisk her off to the airport. Within a few days, he and Loretta were not even bothering to show up for work, preferring instead to spend time together between the satin sheets in the bedroom of the house shared by the mayor and his wife. As it was destined to happen, Mrs. Chacon decided to cut her visit short and bring her mother back with her so they could redecorate the living room. They flew back on Southwest Airlines, ate a few peanuts on the flight and downed a couple of martinis, and landed safely at the airport. A taxi dropped them off in front of her house and they entered through the kitchen. Mrs. Chacon decided to put on a pot of coffee while they unwound from the flight, which had taken much longer than they expected. She kicked her shoes off, and went to the bedroom to get her slippers which were usually on the floor next to her bed, and the rest is history. Barney Sedillo resigned as campaign manager and went back to work for Legal Aid, and Loretta is still wearing a bandana trying to cover the spot originally holding the handful of hair Mrs. Chacon pulled out of her head as she was trying to make a quick exit through the sliding glass door in the mayor's bedroom. It's a little hazy as to whether or not they will be sitting across from each other in divorce court, but we knew the news would eventually get around.

A few weeks later, the three of us sat next to each other at Lala's beauty parlor, each of us in a different stage of preparation for that night's reunion events. I was wiggling under a too-hot hair dryer, while Jolene was trying to eat a bag of chips with newly manicured nails. At the other end of the room, Jolene was maxing out her credit cards on mousse, hair spray and a bikini wax, which for the life of me I couldn't see as necessary, unless she had plans with the UPS guy who had agreed to meet her later in the evening. By seven o'clock that night, we were parked on three barstools in the dimly lit bar of a downtown hotel, sipping on a few healthy-sized Margaritas, looking around to see if we recognized anybody at the adjoining tables. Darlene found those slimming pantyhose, but it seemed everything that wasn't squeezed in was shoved upward, so she was busy trying to cover her more humongous than before spare tire with the black shawl she'd wrapped around her shoulders. She complained that maybe she should have bought the one that squishes you from the top, too. From the look of things, we might have put in a lot of extra effort for nothing, as there had yet to be one single person with whom we had actually interacted in those four years. After an hour or so, people began wandering into the hotel, poking their heads into the now empty bar and heading downstairs to the banquet room. We grabbed our half-empty glasses and decided to join them. There were about a dozen people each of us recognized, so we spent a few minutes mulling over old times and inquiring about what they had been doing for all these years. Billy Williams was still cracking beaner jokes, but had also added blonde jokes to his repertoire, his platinum blonde wife wrinkling her brow each time he started to tell one. Gary Garcia showed up wearing his leather motorcycle jacket, his hair still slicked back in the Fonzie style he had emulated long before Happy Days came to television. Wanda Kinnard was as beautiful as ever. She divorced her high school sweetheart to marry a real estate mogul who treated her like the princess she always wanted to be. They had traveled from their villa in Puerto Vallarta, Mexico just to be here. She was wearing a purple broomstick skirt with a white backless halter top which showed off her seamless tan, and you could sure tell he was crazy about her the way he hung on every word she said while making sure she had everything she needed, rum and Coke included. (None of us were surprised later in the evening when they were elected King and Queen of the festivities.)

There were a few who had survived serious illnesses, and others who were obviously suffering from some unnamed condition, but overall, the evening turned out better than three of us had expected. Of course, a good number of our classmates were retired, having worked for the State for most of their adult lives. A few married well; others had never seen the inside of an office until either they were divorced or widowed. A couple of them were sporting diamonds bigger than their knuckles, hanging on to handsome younger men wearing Armani suits. Darlene conjectured they were probably from the escort service in the adjoining town, and the rings were probably glass or that new material that looked just like diamonds. What was that called ...oh yes, cubic zirconia.

The three of us sat at a table near the front where we had the vantage point of seeing everyone as they checked in at the table next to us. Right off the bat, we saw that whoever was in charge of assigning tables must have been somebody's husband who wasn't in high school with us, because of the first few people who sat down, Jerry Lou Humphrey and Louise Warner ended up sitting right next to each other. They had been mortal enemies all through senior year, Jerry Lou having gotten pregnant with Oscar Baker's baby right after he and Louise broke up. They had just gotten back together when Jerry Lou dropped the bomb on graduation night, and Oscar ended up attending his own shotgun wedding the following month, because her father owned the meat packing plant where his father worked. Ten years and three children later, they divorced and so far Louise had never found anyone else she wanted to marry, although a story circulated around town that she was living with another woman who it was said bought her an awful lot of jewelry at Zale's Jewelers for them to be just roommates. We looked around to see if Oscar had shown up yet, his new thirty-four year old wife in tow. Oscar left town a few years after his divorce from Jerry Lou, but later returned to manage his father's business. It wasn't long before the office tramp set her sights on him, and I guess he just couldn't help himself. The new Mrs. walked down the aisle in a white designer gown, bridal veil and all cascading for twenty feet behind her. The last time I saw Oscar he was talking to my brother at the sporting goods store in the mall. He was trying to suck his gut in and he kept running his fingers through thinning hair. I found it odd that he didn't bother to ask about Louise, being that she had bee the love of his life. Maybe he'd heard the rumors, too.

Alice Egan, who dated most of the football team, walked in wearing enough jewelry around her neck to light a small village, and in strappy heels so high they made her look Amazonian compared to her husband. Out of the corner of my eye I could see Helen Wright stumbling her way into the bar. The three of us simultaneously turned our heads to avoid her, as memories of her had left a sour taste in our mouths for all these years. Helen was a troublemaker from the time she transferred to the high school from a small town in the southern part of the state. Within weeks of her arrival, she had managed to alienate most of the girls in the Junior class. If she couldn't have their boyfriends full time, she could sure have them long enough to teach them a few tricks behind the gymnasium. If there was any guy who hadn't slept with her, he must have been absent the day his turn came around. By graduation day, she had mellowed down enough to become engaged to the assistant coach, John Medina, a union which although frowned upon by the faculty, lasted twenty years longer than it probably should have.

A sticky little rumor continued to circulate over the years that she had been seeing Joe Dayton on the side. He was class president during junior and senior years, and they had dated for a couple of semesters. He went off to college and when he was in his mid-twenties came back and married a woman considerably older than he was—-twenty-five years to be exact. We all figured it was about money since it wasn't long before he and Helen began rendezvousing at the Holiday Inn a couple of Thursdays each month. Helen had a few opportunities to remarry during those years to some fairly decent guys, but she was always fearful that if she did, she might lose her chance to be with Joe in case he ever decided to leave his wife. So she seemed content to sit by the phone waiting for his call, imagining that this might be the day he was going to get a divorce. But he never did. Even though his wife was now in her eighties, he continued to take care of all her needs, doting over her as he helped her in and out of the car. You could count on one hand the few chance encounters he and Helen had, but they must have been enough to keep her going, since surely she could have married that beer-drinking cowboy she danced the night away with more than once at the local Fraternal of Eagles hall. His blue Ford pickup was parked in her driveway often enough in the early hours of the morning as we headed off to work.

We all looked up, startled by the drumroll which filled the room. It was Marilou, walking slowly on the arm of a ruggedly handsome older man, her other hand on a wooden cane. She had been living in Dallas for the past twenty years, and was excited about coming to the reunion. A couple of months before making the trip to the reunion, she decided to have liposuction on her thighs for a quick slimdown, and on the way to the spa, her car was hit by a butter truck, rendering her out of commission for a few weeks. Much to the dismay of most of the men attending, some years ago she underwent breast reduction as her back had been killing her from all those years of lugging her big gazonkas around. Why, now they were hardly bigger than most of ours, so we all went up to say hello, no longer feeling intimidated in her presence.

Later that night when it was all over, I sat in front of the fireplace in my living room, feeling the warmth of the fire on my face and a slight chill which still remained in my head. I pondered what the reason might be why each of us had decided to go to that reunion. Although we joked about wanting to see who had packed the pounds on or who had hooked up with yet another loser, I sensed the reality might be that we wanted to see who had survived the past fifty years. It was half a century, the passing of which was quickly propelling us to the remaining years of our lives. Everyone looked older, whether they wanted to admit it or not. The few who had been under the surgeon's knife might have changed the surface, but their eyes still reflected the inevitable toll of age. As I wrapped the knitted afghan tightly around my shoulders and snuggled closer to my ever-present cat, my eyes misted with the thought that this might have been the last reunion the three of us would attend. A week before the reunion, I received the news that the cancer Jolene had fought so valiantly had returned, and I was having difficulty holding on to that secret until she was ready to tell Darlene.

42

I never thought the day would come when I would admit I was crazy about another female. For almost ten years now I've been keeping company with a sweetheart in her mid-sixties. She's got the biggest brown eyes you ever wanna see, with eyelashes out to here. She's got short black hair with a touch of white, always needing a handful of gel to keep it in place.

I've had a few relationships in my life; some worked, some didn't. It all had to do with chemistry, a mutual attraction fueled by a strong desire to be part of a couple. I met this gorgeous creature while driving down the highway one sunny afternoon. I don't usually pick up strangers, but I was a little lonely, and those big brown eyes were looking at me with such possibilities. I just couldn't help myself. So we've been carrying on for all these years now, and most of my close friends bless our relationship. We've both aged a little, a few more white hairs here and there and a little slower gait.

I can tell her all my problems, or how my day is going, and she listens intently while I bitch about the weather, the traffic, or the cost of gasoline. She never makes me feel like I'm hogging the conversation. She's usually a person of few words, but oh, can she make you feel special! Pushing the door open before I get there, making sure I have my newspaper with my breakfast, and when she's feeling lovey-dovey, she gently nuzzles my neck. When my mother saw her the first time, she only said, "She's black! You won't be able to see her at night! I don't know what you're going to tell your father..." How rude, I think, they didn't even give her a chance to get to know them.

As I glance over at her, I want to tell her of my deep love, of how precious these years have been, and that we're not getting any younger. We need to shout it out to the world! I want to tell her of all the times I've appreciated it when she puts her head on my shoulder when I'm in tears and comforts me when it seems as though there is no comfort.

But I see she's preoccupied. She's out in the middle of the yard, rolling in the grass, her legs pointed toward Heaven. How unladylike, but on her it looks good. She knows I'm there, so she starts to show off, running around the yard in a big circle, herding the flock of sheep visible only in the imagination of the true Border Collie. Round and round my Chucky runs, until she gets the imaginary sheep lined up. Then she comes over to me, expecting the dog biscuit she's become accustomed to, not only from me but from every business in the city. I laugh and tell her she's spoiled, but these are words foreign to her, so she licks my hand instead. The third biscuit she takes into the extra bedroom and gently sets it in a corner, and, thinking I'm not watching, proceeds to push layers of imaginary dirt over it with her nose, making sure it's well hidden until she needs another snack.

I'm hoping this love of my life will be with me for many more years, but for the meantime, I'm content to wake up each morning as she gently puts her paw on my pillow, making sure I know it's time to get up.

(Postscript: Chucky went up to Dog Heaven on January 26, 2007, leaving me a small shrine of dog biscuits assembled in a circle in the middle of the living room.)

43

How does one describe *la familia*. Is it *la comida, los abuelos, mis hermanos y hermanas, mis padres?*

Is it *el barrio, las casas, la génte?*

Is it *la iglesia, nuestra fé?*

Is it what we've done or what we need to do? Is it all of this entangled into the web of the spider?

Is it their eyes, the color of piñon nuts, that sparkle with joy, and from which *lagrimas* flow like a river on every sad or happy occasion?

Or is it refuge, a place para *llorar;* a place para *cantár,* a place para *gritár?*

Is it the safety of the *Madre's* arms, which cradle with softness and affection, the gentle touch? Is it the acceptance of all your wins and all your losses, your ups and downs, your highs and lows?

Is it the aroma of the kitchen, the melody of the voices mixed in harmony?

Los altares, the shrines, the prayers.

La inocencia, the naiveté.

Los cuéntos, las estorias, los chistés, the legends.

Or is it the smell of mothballs on *Abuelita's* old fur coat that she wears only on special occasions?

And if you put it all together and mix it with a little *cerveza,* isn't it *all* familia?

Marie Romero Cash

by
Kay Lockridge

The sobriquet may have become a cliché, but Marie Romero Cash truly is a Renaissance woman. As an author, and well-known for creating exquisite, award-winning santos (retablos and bultos), Romero Cash says she and her art are constantly evolving.

"I started off as a santera," Romero Cash said, "and then I branched out to a folk art focus. Since then, I have evolved to writing as a way to express my experiences and vision. I am not a 'jack-of-all-trades, master of none,' because I put my all into everything I do." Many of her pieces have contemporary subjects using traditional techniques and natural dye paints.

Romero Cash, who described herself as a 'late-bloomer,' started college at the age of 50 and went on to earn a bachelor's degree in Southwestern studies and continued her studies at the University of New Mexico and the College of Santa Fe. Her published books include *Tortilla Chronicles: Growing Up in Santa Fe*, *Santos* and this collection of short stories, *Lowrider Blues: Cantando, Gritando y Llorando* (Stories from my Inner Barrio), the last two from Sunstone Press.

"Memoirs suggest we lead parallel lives with one another," Romero Cash said. "No matter where you come from, no matter what your experiences, we are more alike than different. That's why I think my work has resonance with so many people."

Romero Cash joined her sister, award-winning artist Anita Romero Jones, at Spanish Market in 1974, a time when they were two of only four santeras at the market (Gloria Lopez and Monica Sosaya Halford were the other two). She said she sees progress for women over the more than 30 years since then, suggesting that half of the santeros working today are women.

"I'm not a feminist, but it has been women who have been most supportive of me and my work over the years," Romero Cash said with conviction. "I've been married twice and raised three wonderful children, but my needs have changed. People pay me to create, not to do laundry.

"I guess I've always gone against the grain. If something was not working, such as a marriage, I would not stay in it. The same goes for my art. If I need to do something else, I will. I am still looking for career alternatives."

Romero Cash makes no bones about it: she is a woman who creates art for a living, and it's not easy. "Art is an expendable commodity; it's one of the first things to be cut—whether in school or in business—in hard times. It's tough to be an artist," Romero Cash added.

Yet, Romero Cash was adamant that this is what she must do. It wasn't always that way. She is the daughter of the late Emilio and Senaida Romero, who also began their collaboration in tinsmithing and Colcha embroidery later in life after Emilio's retirement from Los Alamos National Laboratory. Romero Cash first entered the world of business as a legal secretary. She was in her early thirties when she turned to art and has never looked back.

A very personal aspect of her art has been the creation of shrines to her late family members. What began as a home shrine evolved into installations at both the Museum of International Folk Art and the Palace of the Governors in Santa Fe.

"Shrines take on lives of their own," Romero Cash noted. "They open up your life and thoughts. The one displayed at the Folk Art Museum began as a home shrine years ago and things kept happening...and, it (the shrine) grew."

It first was shown at the Frost Museum in Miami. In the meantime, Tey Marianna Nunn, then the curator at the Museum of Folk Art, suggested that the Santa Fe museum would be the perfect place for it to be shown.

Nunn, now the director and chief curator of the visual arts program at the National Hispanic Cultural Center in Albuquerque, said the shrine reflects Romero Cash's "endless talent and search for creativity and space. For a woman, altar making is a recognized art since the 1970s. Installation art is woman's art, personal art, religious art.

"Hispana, Latina and Chicana artists have been at the forefront of this movement, (sensing) an artistic and cultural need to express themselves," Nunn said. "I always liked the idea of taking bits and pieces (of life) and adding them to a larger piece of art. Shrines express this."

While such installations often are called altars, Romero Cash said she preferred the word 'shrine' rather than 'altar,' "because I consider an altar to be primarily devotional and a shrine to be more of remembrance.

"Shrines are part of Americana, an authentic way of life. I think it (the shrine currently at the museum) belongs at the Smithsonian Institution in Washington, where it could speak to all Americans," Romero Cash said.

"I guess I'm kind of a Grandma Moses at this point. Like her, I started my art later in life, yet I keep looking ahead. My two sisters and three brothers all create art in some way, and my son (the painter Gregory Lomayesva) has followed in my footsteps. One of my daughters used to do straw work, but both are in retail (now). My grandson, Anthony, pursues his own art in web design at the Albuquerque Art Academy.

"My bottom line is that I love to delight the viewer.... I do pieces that are creative, fun and a delight to look at. When someone looks at my work and their eyes light up in awe, this is sustenance for my soul," Romero Cash said.

GLOSSARY

A la machina (ma -kee-nah) – holy smokes! Oh my gosh!

Abuelita – grandmother

Abuelo – grandfather

Altares – altars, shrines

Amiga – female friend

Atole – gruel made from blue corn flour

Barrió – neighborhood

Beaner – person who eats a lot of beans, slang for Hispanic person

Biscochitos – sugar cookies

Borracho – drunk

Búrque – slang for Albuquerque

Calma té – calm down

Cantar – sing

Carnal – slang for relative

Cerveza – beer

Chicas locas – crazy chicks

Chistes – gossip, stories spread by word of mouth

Chollos – wannabee gang members wearing bandanas wrapped around
    their heads

Chuco – slang for Pachuco

Cojones (ko-ho-nes)– testicles, balls

Cuentos – tales, stories

Dios Mío – My God

Esperanza – hope

Estorias – stories

Fajitas – marinated meat strips

Familia – family

Fé – faith

Gargaho – spitball

Gente – people

Gracias a Dios – thanks be to God

Greñuda – messy haired girl

Gringa – anglo woman

Gringo – anglo

Gritar – holler

Hermanas –sisters

Hermanos – brothers

Hombre – man

Iglesia – church

Illumbran – illuminate

La Clinica – the medical clinic

La Conquistadora – patroness of St. Francis Cathedral Basilica in Santa Fe

Lágrimas – tears

Las Ricas – rich women

Llorar – cry

Machó – overly male

Madrecita – mother

Marijuano – pothead

Mi hito – my son

Mijo – mi hijo – my son

Mira – look

Musicos – musicians

Nuestra fé – our faith

Ojo de la Vaca – Cow Springs

Pachuco – slang term for zoot suiter, one with slicked back hair, pegged
    pants

Padre Nuestro – Our Father

Padres – parents

Pobrecita – poor her

Pobrecito – poor him

Que va – my goodness

Ruega por nosotros – Pray for us

Salsa – hot sauce

Santa Maria, Madre de Dios – Hail Mary, Full of Grace

Stúpida – stupid (fem.)

Taquitos – rolled tacos

Tia – aunt

Tio – uncle

Todas perfumadas – wearing too much perfume

Valse – waltz

Vato – guy (slang)

Velas – candles

Vieja – old woman, wife

Viejo – old man, my husband